by Adèle De Leeuw

THE PATCHWORK QUILT
NOBODY'S DOLL
BLUE RIBBONS FOR MEG
DONNY

by Adèle and Cateau De Leeuw

MICKEY THE MONKEY
HIDEAWAY HOUSE
THE EXPANDABLE BROWNS
THE CABOOSE CLUB

The Caboose Club

The
Caboose
Club

by

Adèle and Cateau De Leeuw

ILLUSTRATED BY DON SIBLEY

Little, Brown and Company
Boston · Toronto

*Published simultaneously in Canada
by Little, Brown & Company (Canada) Limited*

PRINTED IN THE UNITED STATES OF AMERICA

To Philip M. Kelly
who, without realizing it, started us on this book —
and then furnished us with valuable information.

Acknowledgment

The authors gratefully acknowledge the help given them by Frederick Deibert, owner of the Model Railroad Shop in New Market, New Jersey, whose "pike" was an inspiration.

The Caboose Club

CHAPTER 1

It all started with Bob's Christmas gift from Mr. Teague.

Christmas was always a wonderful day at the Browns'. They began to celebrate early in the morning, before it was light, because Suzie, who was five, wanted to see if she could catch Santa Claus. By nine o'clock they felt as if they had been up all day. Papers littered the floor, ribbons and tinsel string were everywhere, and the presents, without their wrappings, were ranged under the tree.

They were all making so much noise that they scarcely heard the doorbell.

Suzie cried, "Maybe it's Santa Claus come back!" and, leading her new duck on a string, managed to get there first. It wasn't Santa Claus, after all, only Mr. Teague and his wife.

"Mr. Teague, look, look! I asked for a duck and he brought me a duck! His name's Doctor Quack and he talks!"

Mr. Teague had been their boarder when he and his wife were separated for a while. Since then he had come out to the house several times, "because it showed me what a real

3

home could be like," he said, and to show them Mrs. Teague, who was very pretty.

"And besides, he likes Mom's cooking," Bob said. Even when Mr. Teague had been so glum that he would scarcely talk at all, he had done well by Mother's cooking.

He picked up Suzie now and swung her high. She still held on to her duck, however. Mrs. Teague had an armful of presents. Bob and Pat and Suzie tried not to look too interested, but the shapes were exciting.

Father and Mother came into the hall, holding out their hands in welcome. "Come in, come in! You're in time for the windup!"

Rex skittered around a corner and leaped upon the visitors like old friends. He was wearing a huge red bow that had gone lopsided, and Pat had drawn a wreath of holly berries and leaves on paper and pasted it onto his collar.

Catten and two of her kittens were playing under the tree. "It's the biggest tree we could find at the nursery!" Pat said proudly, shaking her red braids. "We had to cut off nearly two feet to get it in. Isn't it beautiful?"

Mrs. Teague was staring at it as if she had never seen a Christmas tree before. "See the little angel at the top?" Suzie demanded. "That's supposed to be me."

"Only Suzie is no angel," Bob said swiftly. "Everybody knows that."

Mr. Teague was beaming. "Frances, shall we give them their gifts?"

4

"No, you must see our other presents first, and then watch us open yours," Pat decided. That way it would last longer.

Suzie's turn came first. They let her show her presents because she would have done it anyhow, and, besides, she was the youngest. Father had made her a doll house. "That was what he was doing nights in the cellar!" Suzie said proudly. "And I'm going to have my dolls in it and maybe the kittens."

Father had given Mother a pretty pullover and cardigan set, Mother had given Father an electric hand tool. Bob couldn't resist that. "Oh boy, could I use it!" he cried at intervals, looking at it with longing. It was the sort of thing *he* had wanted . . . and he couldn't help being a bit disappointed over his windbreaker. But he was sure his father would let him use the tool now and then; he knew how to take care of tools, and there were so many things he wanted to make.

Pat was ecstatic over Bob's present to her — a handsome box for all her paints. She had a brand-new set of real lettering pens, too, and her mind was full of signs she was going to letter. The house was littered with signs now, but there was always room for one more, and some occasion was always arising that really required a sign.

"Aunt Meg and Uncle Bill were out early this morning," Bob explained, "and brought us all kinds of things, and some money. They're going to meet us at church and come back here to Christmas dinner."

"Something smells awfully good now," Mr. Teague said

eagerly. "I'm so glad you invited us, too." He turned to Mrs. Brown. "You're sure it won't be too much having my friend Wayne Kendall? He's lonesome on Christmas Day, and he's tired of hotel food."

"Christmas is a day for sharing," Mother said. "The more the merrier — as long as the table stretches."

They showed the Teagues everything . . . and then, at last, they could open the exciting-looking presents. Bob, throwing tissue paper right and left, let out a whoop. "Gee, Mr. Teague! This is swell! Now maybe I've *got* to use Dad's tool!"

It was a double present, really — do-it-yourself kits for a boxcar and a caboose, in HO gauge, made to scale for a model railroad. Bob had once had a little electric train of tinplate, but that had long since been discarded because he was too old for it; and anyhow, the children in Mother's nursery school had pretty well battered it up. But these were different; these were the kind that grown men worked on.

"I knew well enough," Mr. Teague said proudly, "that you were forever making something while I was here, and doing a mighty good job. I thought you'd like to tackle something like this."

Pat was leaping around like a whirling dervish showing off her red stole and matching mittens. Just because she had red hair people seemed to think she shouldn't wear red — and it was her favorite color. She gave Mrs. Teague a bear hug, and tripped over Suzie, who was looking more angelic than

6

usual in a white angora beret and little white tippet. Mrs. Teague had made all of them.

When it was time for church they had to shut Doctor Quack up in the cellar. "He's got to have a bed of his own," Suzie announced firmly. "I'll make it when I get back."

She walked backward to the car, calling, "Good-by, house, good-by tree, good-by Catten and Rex, good-by Doctor Quack!"

"But why," Mrs. Teague asked, "do you call him Doctor Quack? I should have thought you'd name him Donald."

"Oh no," Suzie said easily. "That's like lots of ducks. This one is special." She looked up prettily at Mrs. Teague bending above her. "The doctor is a quack, so this is Doctor Quack."

"Suzie!" said Mother, who had overheard. "How can you say a thing like that about our dear Doctor Hibbard?"

"Not Doctor Hibbard," Suzie said. "But that lady who was at our house the other day said, 'The doctor is a —'"

"Well, the *duck* may be a quack," Mother put in hurriedly, "but don't let me hear you calling Doctor Hibbard that. Are we all here?" she counted noses. "Then let's go, I'm afraid we're late."

The church was glowing with light that streamed through the tall windows, and fragrant with pine boughs and flowers. The organ was playing softly, and a hush lay over the congregation. Bob and Pat bent their heads, and even Suzie was quiet and thoughtful. Bob had a smoothed-out, warm

7

feeling. It was good to be here with the family and the Teagues and Aunt Meg and Uncle Bill Jarvis, celebrating this special day of the year together. Christmas was more than presents and fun. It was this hour, too, and the way it made you feel inside, and the thoughts it started in your head. He stood up and shouted lustily:

Noël, Noël, Noël, Noël,
Born is the King of Is-ra-el!

Everybody had a tremendous appetite for dinner. Bob was eager to get at his kits, but it was hard to keep your mind on *anything* when such smells were wafting through the house. Besides, he had to help set chairs around and fill water glasses and wash up pans. His mother's face was flushed, little locks of her bright red hair curled over her ears, and he thought again how pretty she was. And fun! Nobody's mother was as much fun as his mother was!

Pat had made a centerpiece of fruits and vegetables, and the flowers Uncle Bill had brought were on the sideboard. Bob thought proudly that he and his father and Uncle Bill had done a good job of refinishing the dining-room set. They had bought it for twenty-five dollars at a country auction. He remembered how crowded they had been in the dinette of the little green house they lived in before. Now they could put two leaves in the big round table and still have room!

Mother said grace, and then Father brought in the turkey. Aunt Meg served the vegetables, and Pat the cranberry

8

sauce and gravy, and Mr. Teague lit the candles. Mr. Kendall kept asking if he couldn't do something, but they told him he was their special guest.

"After you've been here a couple of times, we'll let you work," Bob told him, and Mr. Kendall laughed. "Then I'll *really* feel at home."

Mr. Kendall had a continual beam on his face. His eyes shone in the candlelight and he kept saying, "You don't know how much it means to me to be with a family — and such a family — on this day!"

He was different from Mr. Teague, his friend. Mr. Teague was short and stocky and dark and inclined to be quiet. But Mr. Kendall was tall and rangy, with long arms and legs, and sparkling blue eyes and a mop of fair hair, and he liked to talk. He had one thing in common with Mr. Teague, though. He liked Mother's cooking. He ate huge portions of everything, and took seconds, and even thirds of the dessert, which was two kinds of pie with ice cream.

Pat threw herself back in her chair and fanned herself with her braids.

"I'm absolutely stuffed," she announced.

"You look it," Bob told her, still spooning up the last of his ice cream. "You've popped a button."

"Where?" Pat demanded, looking down in alarm.

"April Fool — ahead of time," Bob said, grinning. Last year Pat had caught *him* on April Fool's Day, and now he had paid her back.

"This was the best dinner I've ever eaten anywhere," Mr. Teague said strongly.

"Not only the best dinner," Uncle Bill said, "but the best company." He was holding Aunt Meg's hand and smiling at her. "I was the luckiest man in the world to marry into this family."

Bob said, surprisingly, "We were lucky, too." Uncle Bill was nice to have around . . . jolly and full of fun, and he could do lots of things. All at once he remembered. "Hey, Uncle Bill! You can be a lot of help to me!"

Uncle Bill grinned. "Glad I have my uses," he said. "What's up?"

"I was just thinking," Bob said hurriedly, "that when I put together my boxcar and caboose, I'll have to know a lot about railroads, and you have that new job with a railroad —"

"Only in the engineering department," Uncle Bill said. "Yes, but you could find out."

"I guess I can manage to keep one jump ahead of you," Uncle Bill offered, "if I try hard. Just be sure to tell me a day in advance what's bothering you so I can hunt it up!" He liked to joke, but Bob felt relieved. Uncle Bill wouldn't fail him.

He was awfully anxious to get going on the construction . . . at least to spread out the parts and see what he had to do. When there was anything to make, his fingers fairly itched.

After dinner they all felt too pleasantly full to move. But

there were dishes to wash, and Bob had his job cut out for him. In the midst of it he heard Pat shriek, "The tree! The tree's coming down!"

He dashed into the living room. The huge Christmas tree was shaking as if it were in a strong wind, and the ornaments were bobbing crazily. Mr. Kendall thrust one of his long arms into the branches and grabbed the trunk, holding it steady, while the others rushed to brace it up.

Suzie cried, "It's Catten's kitten!" And sure enough, there was Misty in one of the topmost branches, batting happily at the tinsel strings. While they watched, several of the gay balls fell to the floor with a tinkling sound.

"Oh — oh!" Suzie mourned. "They were so pretty!"

Rex came loping into the room to see what all the excitement was about. He raced around the tree, barking with excitement and slapping them with his long tail, and that knocked two more ornaments off. The floor was sprinkled with bits of colored glass.

Suzie cried, "Rex, Rex! Come here."

But when he turned to obey he stepped into the crushed glass and let out a funny little howl. Suzie scarcely knew which way to turn — it was her kitten that had caused all the trouble, and her beloved Rex that had cut his foot. She decided on Rex, because the family was coaxing the kitten down, and Bob had gone for a stepladder. So she took Rex with her to the bathroom to wash his foot and put on a Band-Aid.

Aunt Meg brought a dustpan and began sweeping up the bits of glass and tinsel. Mrs. Teague said, "It would have been dreadful if anything had happened to the tree. It really is the most beautiful tree I've seen."

"Aren't Christmas trees fun?" Pat asked.

"I never had a Christmas tree," Mrs. Teague said quite softly.

Pat could scarcely believe her ears. "Never? Not even when you were little?"

"Never," said Mrs. Teague. "I always knew that I was missing something very special, but now I know it even more."

Pat and Bob exchanged glances of pity. Imagine having to live in a household like that — where they didn't make much of Christmas. Why, it would be dreadful!

Maybe, Bob thought, that was one of the reasons Mr. and Mrs. Teague had separated, for a while. Mr. Teague had been an only child, and if Mrs. Teague had never had Christmas trees when she was young . . .

After order was restored, Mr. Kendall got down on the floor to play with Suzie and her doll's house. The dishes finally were washed and put away. Mrs. Brown brought out some Christmas punch she had made, and they all gathered around the piano and sang the carols they loved best.

At last it was time for the guests to go home. Nobody seemed to want to go, but Bob was beginning to wish they *would* go. He could hardly start work on his railroad kits while they were there, and he didn't want to wait much longer to begin. Why, the day was nearly over!

Mrs. Teague said, with tears in her eyes, "Thank you for a *beautiful* time!" and Mr. Kendall said, "May I come back?"

Mother said in a warm voice, "Whenever you get lonely, or you're tired of hotel food —"

"I'm afraid you're going to see me pretty often," Mr. Kendall threatened happily.

Uncle Bill put Aunt Meg's coat on as if she were a Dresden china figure and would break, and tied her scarf over her hair. "Come along, darling, we have a home of our own."

"Thank you for all the presents, Aunt Meg," Bob and Pat said, almost with one voice. "And we sure can use the money!" Bob had his practically spent already . . . he knew just what he was going to buy.

Suzie took Doctor Quack off to bed him down in the barn, and Rex went trotting after, hardly limping at all, and very proud of his Band-Aid. Pat settled down to make a sign, Danger — Glass, to put under the tree, she said, but everybody knew she was just anxious to try out her new lettering pens.

"When I get that done," she said importantly, "I think I'll make one for the duck. If he's a doctor, he ought to have office hours!"

Mother and Dad were washing up. At last there was a chance to get going on some part of the new outfit. Bob spread out the pieces and smoothed the sheet of directions. There was a lot of filing to do; he could see that. Maybe he'd better wait for his father to show him how to use the new tool so he could grind off excess metal on some of the parts when he had tweaked off the flash. He wouldn't want to spoil anything! He began reading the directions, muttering under his breath.

It all sounded like gibberish to Pat. She said, her head bent over the cardboard she was lettering, "What's a bushing, for Pete's sake?"

Bob said, still reading, "Why, anybody knows what a bushing is, silly."

"Well, I don't and I'm somebody," Pat flashed back. "Do you?"

"Sure."

"What is it, then?"

"It's a lining for a hole, and made of metal or plastic, and you can take it out if you want to."

"What's it for?"

"You need a bushing," Bob explained patiently, "to keep down friction. To keep one piece of metal from rubbing against another. In this case, to insulate the caboose from the electricity in the rails. Or sometimes you just use a bushing to make a hole smaller."

Pat sat back. "Well, if you want to make a hole smaller, why don't you make it smaller in the first place, without having to put another piece of metal in it?"

Bob said disgustedly, "Golly! Girls!" He went on reading, half aloud.

After a while she couldn't keep from asking, "And what's a catwalk?"

"What does it sound like?" he returned.

"A little narrow walk, just big enough for a cat?"

"Sort of. It's on top of a freight car. It connects the roof-walk with the ladder, so the brakeman can get up on top."

"How do you know all these things?"

"I read and ask questions," he returned. "Look, here's a picture of what I'm going to make." He spread out the sheet of instructions; already it looked as if he had been handling it for days.

"This is the caboose. I think I'll make that first."

Pat looked at the careful drawings. "Oh," she cried, "that's the little house that goes on the end of freight trains!"

"Sure."

"Wouldn't it be fun to *live* in one?" Pat clasped her hands together.

"Live in one what?" Father asked, coming in from the kitchen.

"A caboose. It's darling . . . with those little porches and the — the sort of flat tower on top where you could climb up and sit —"

"Cupola," Bob corrected, from his superior knowledge.

"*Umm*," said Father. "No, thanks. We bought this place so we'd have some room to move around in. A caboose would be considerably smaller than our old house, and that was too small."

He stood in the doorway between the rooms and looked around happily. "Come on, chickens, it's time for *The Littlest Angel*. The first time in this house . . . our first Christmas in this house."

Suzie came with Rex. Mother had slipped into the yellow pullover and cardigan Father had given her, and her eyes were sparkling.

"This is the best part of the whole day," she said softly.

They gathered around the fireplace. Bob built up the fire, Pat brought the dish of nuts. Father got the book down from the bookshelves, and Suzie climbed onto his lap. The tree lights winked in the dusk, Bob lit a standing lamp and crouched on the rug at his father's feet.

Father began to read in his deep resonant voice, " 'Once upon a time — oh, many, many years ago as time is calculated by men — but which was only Yesterday in the Celestial Calendar of Heaven . . .' "

It had been a wonderful day, Bob thought. And, still listening to his father's voice telling the familiar story, he couldn't help thinking, And tomorrow — and tomorrow — and tomorrow . . .

CHAPTER 2

Next day Russell Skinner came in to compare notes. He was examining the caboose kit when Orphie Sparks dropped by.

"I wish I'd got something like this," Skinny said, trying not to sound wistful. "I know a man who's a model railroad fan, and Pop took me over a couple of times to see his pike —"

"He did?" Bob said eagerly. "What's it like?" He hadn't known that a model railroad was called a pike, until yesterday, but now the word came naturally.

"He has it laid out in his sun parlor." Skinny obliged with details. "Gosh, it's a real outfit! Tunnels and signal towers, and mountains and a quarry and a lumberyard and a factory, and bridges, and even a turntable —"

"A turntable!" Bob and Orphie said together. "That must have been a special job!"

"He made everything himself," Skinny said. "It's taken him years and he's not done yet. He has diesels and old-style locomotives, and dozens of freight cars and tank cars, and gondolas and passenger cars and cranes, and those things on the tracks that they run the cars onto to uncouple 'em. What do you call 'em? . . . Oh, I know — ramps."

Orphie's dark face was alive with interest. "I guess I'm crazy about model railroads because my father used to be a porter on a real one. He earned money to go to college that way, and he knows all about 'em," Orphie said proudly.

Mr. Sparks was a history teacher in the high school at Woodcrest. That was not too different from lots of other people. But not everybody was lucky enough to have a father who had once been a Pullman porter! Orphie was a nice guy to know.

"Hi!" Chip Randolph said from the doorway. He was carrying a new basketball under his arm.

"You got it!" the others cried, with one voice. "Say, Chip, it's a beaut!"

"Sure I got it," Chip said, with his assured air. He tossed his head. "I always get what I ask for." He looked at them meaningfully. "And I asked for plenty this year!" His quick eyes swept over the card table where Bob had laid out the tiny parts of the caboose. "What's that?"

Orphie said eagerly, "It's a caboose. . . . You know, the end car of a freight train."

"You still playing with trains?" Chip said derisively. "I gave that up years ago."

Bob snapped, "This isn't playing with them, sap, this is making them. It's just like the real thing — every part is to scale."

19

"*Umm,*" Chip said, turning away. "Come on, want to practice some shots?"

It was too good a chance to miss. They trooped outdoors with Chip, and since it was his ball, let him make the first pass at the basket fixed to the side of the barn.

Kenny Grainger came through the hedge. Even after nearly a year of putting up with Kenny, Bob had all he could do not to groan. Kenny was a pest. He was an only child, and spoiled, and he found life at the Browns' so entrancing that he came over on all occasions, and much too often in between. They had tried various ways of discouraging him, but Kenny was not to be discouraged. To make matters worse, he was younger than Bob and Bob's particular friends, but he refused to let that bother him.

"Hello," he said brightly. "I want to play, too."

"You're too short."

"I can try, can't I? Come on, let me try."

Bob handed over the ball with a grunt, and Kenny hoisted it up in the air and gave a mighty heave. It fell far short of the basket — and right in front of Doctor Quack, who had waddled out of the barn without their noticing him. The ball bounced off the ground, and Doctor Quack turned indignantly to the nearest person — who was Chip — and nipped him on the ankle.

"Hey!" Chip yelled. You would have thought the Indians were after him. He hopped about on his good foot, his face screwed up, yelling all the while. "I bet I've been bitten right

to the bone! Where'd you get that blamed duck, anyhow?"

"Aw, you're just a crybaby!" Kenny said loudly. Bob stared at him. If ever there was a crybaby, it was Kenny. "He wouldn't hurt anybody," Kenny said. "He's just a little old duck. See? He wouldn't hurt anybody." And he offered his hand to the Doctor. The Doctor promptly nipped it.

Kenny yelled louder than Chip, and held up his hand as if there were a stream of blood running from it. His eyes were big and frightened. "I'm bitten, I'm bitten! Take your duck away, he bit me!"

Suzie heard the commotion and came running. "You stop bothering my duck!" she cried. Her eyes flashed from one boy to the other. "You great big boys bothering my poor little Doctor Quack! Go away!"

"He bit me!" Chip said in an aggrieved tone.

"And me!" Kenny added. "*You* take *him* away!"

"Doctor Quack wants to be outside a while, so *you* can go inside," Suzie said firmly.

"Aw, come on, then," Bob said. He knew better than to argue with Suzie — at times. "We'll go in the house again and work on the caboose." Chip took his basketball and decided he'd go home. Skinny left, too. But Orphie and Kenny stayed.

Bob wished Kenny would go home, but Kenny never went home until he was practically pushed. He hung over the table now, handling all the tiny parts, picking each one up and scrutinizing it and asking what it was and where it went. Bob was afraid he would drop something on the floor and lose it, but Kenny said loftily that he was the most careful person he knew of. He never lost anything — almost never, that is.

Orphie was different. He handled the parts with care and knowledge. Bob would have loved to work on the caboose entirely by himself . . . because then it would take longer and he could enjoy all of it. But Orphie was a good workman and he might be very helpful — knowing about railroads as he did.

They had barely settled down to a little construction work when Skinny came back, bringing Clint Snow. "I met Clint," Skinny said breathlessly, "and he wanted to see your kit."

Clint Snow was a tall boy who was older than most of the gang. He liked to be one of them, though, because it gave him a chance to boss them. Most of the time they didn't mind; they did as they pleased anyhow.

He got all steamed up about the caboose kit. "I'll bet I could make one of those in no time flat!" he cried. "I'd like to try it."

"Try it," Bob said succinctly. "But not on mine."

"Well, you'll let me work on it, won't you?"

"I don't know. I want to do it all myself — most all, anyhow," he added in some haste, seeing how Orphie looked.

"It ought to be easy."

23

"It's not. . . . It's fun, though," Bob said stoutly. "Everything has to fit — just so."

"Well, if you get stuck, let me know — I can probably help you out!"

Bob grinned inwardly. That sounded like Clint.

Clint leaned across the table, hardly able to keep his fingers off the array of small parts. "What are you going to do with it when you finish it?"

"I'm not going to give it to you, that's one thing sure!" Bob laughed. He filed industriously on the cover plate for a coupler. "Skinny was telling us about a man his father knows who has a whole pike of his own. . . . Tell about it, Skinny."

Skinny was quite willing to go into details. It sounded even better than the last time. Bob declared, "I've got to see that!"

"Why don't we all go?" Skinny asked reasonably. "My father would take us. It would give him a chance to look at it again, too."

"That's a deal," Bob said. "You ask him about a date." He looked up, his eyes lighting with a sudden idea. "Listen," he cried, "why don't we . . ." Then he thought of Kenny. "Why don't you go on home now, Kenny?"

To his surprise Kenny said, "I guess I will." In the doorway he turned. "But I'll be back — tomorrow."

"Oh, sure," Bob said grimly. When he had heard Kenny clatter down the front steps he said to the other boys, "What

I was going to say was, why don't we make a pike ourselves? We *could*. I'd make one by myself, but I think it would be more fun having a bunch of us working on it together. I've got this much to start with, and some of my old tin plate road —"

"Boy!" said Skinny. "I'd like that. Would you, Orphie?"

"Would I!" Orphie said with quiet emphasis. There was no doubt about it.

Clint didn't say anything.

"There's a lot we don't know —" Bob began.

"I could get a book at the library," Orphie said with eagerness. "I bet they have one that tells just what to do."

"And we could ask around," Skinny said helpfully. "Your father and uncle, and my father —"

"And mine," Orphie put in.

"And Mr. Yerkes, who has the pike I was telling about —" Skinny went on.

"We could use the transformers out of our old electric trains," Bob said, thinking aloud. "That would be a big help. And maybe some other stuff. . . . We wouldn't know exactly till we got a line on the pike we wanted to build."

They were all talking at once, all full of ideas and suggestions, when Pat came storming into the room. "What's all the racket?" she demanded. She looked over Bob's shoulder. "You mean to say that's all you've done so far?"

"Well, gosh," he said in an injured voice, "if you tried this you would know it doesn't go fast. You have to be awfully careful not to bend or break things and you have to fit them together exactly right —"

"Just the same, I don't think you've got very far. . . . Where's Suzie?"

"Airing Doctor Quack," Bob said, grinning in spite of himself. "Doctor Quack needed the whole yard, so we came in."

"Mother said to tell you it's time to set the table," Pat told him. The other boys took the hint and scrambled up.

"I'll stop off for the book on my way home," Orphie volunteered.

"And we'll all hunt up whatever stuff we have . . . so we know what we can do in the beginning."

"I'll call you as soon as Pop sets a date," Skinny promised.

It was only three days later that they went to see Mr. Yerkes's pike. Clint had something else to do, but they didn't miss him. It was everything Skinny had said it was, and then some. Bob could almost feel his eyes bulging. From the little he had done he realized how much time and care and thought had gone into the elaborate pike they were looking at. Mr. Yerkes was an enthusiast. He talked their heads off about his outfit . . . but he was full of good common sense, too.

"Maybe you oughtn't to look at such a complete one first," he said, smiling. "Might discourage you. . . . On the other hand, you see what you can work up to — given a couple of hundred years!"

He sat on a high stool in front of his control board. It had several rows of buttons on it in different colors. Signals flashed, trains ran through tunnels and emerged to cross a bridge, their windows lighted like real passenger cars; smoke came out of the locomotives, cars were shunted from one switch to another, and along the road were two small towns, farmland, hills with quarries, a lumberyard, and a coal mine. At the last he ran one of the trains onto the turntable, uncoupled the engine, turned it around and coupled it to another train which had been brought up by a switcher. The boys stood with their mouths agape. It had everything.

"It — it must have cost a lot," Bob said at last.

"A young fortune," Mr. Yerkes said cheerfully. "But you don't have to start out like this."

Skinny gave a hollow laugh. "I should say not. Maybe we can't start out at all."

"Yes, we can," Orphie said stoutly. "That book I got says you can. It's got plans for tracks, and how to build buildings and mountains, and all the rest . . . and it tells how much you need and how to make things. Wait till you see it!"

It was true. The book, which they pored over next day at Bob's, got them all steamed up again. It didn't sound simple . . . but it sounded possible. They could start small, they could make scenery and buildings themselves; they could make everything, in fact, if they really wanted to. The author suggested that the best way was to get a few boys together who were interested in making a pike, and to form a club — an informal sort of club, so they could work together and pool their resources and their money.

"Let's!" Bob said with a shout. "Let's call ourselves the — the —" Suddenly he had it. "The Caboose Club!"

"Sure, the Caboose Club!" they echoed. The name struck them as funny — and right. It stuck. They had a name, a caboose, a freight car, a few tin plate cars and a couple of transformers. It wasn't much — but after all, this was just the beginning.

They took turns reading aloud from the book and making notes. First of all they would get some plywood to make a table top on which to lay out their pike.

"Yes, but where will we put it?" Skinny asked, looking around the living room. "Your mother wouldn't want —"

"Down cellar," Bob said at once. "We've got a big cellar. There's a lot of junk in it, of course, but there's plenty of room. Mom wouldn't mind if we worked down there. And there's a light and everything."

"Besides, it's near the furnace," Orphie laughed. "That's what we need for winter work."

They chipped in to buy the plywood, and Uncle Bill, when he heard of it, came over one evening with six feet of flexible track.

"How much?" Bob demanded.

But Uncle Bill said it was a present. "A dollar and a half's worth of present," he laughed. "I'm telling you so you know what you have to pay out for more of same."

Skinny had got a catalog of parts and equipment from the hobby shop in Woodcrest. It made their mouths water to read of all the stuff you *could* have, if you had the money. First of all, however, they built the table. There was a sketch in the book to show them just how to go about it. It was a sturdy affair, strong enough to carry a real outfit, and well braced. Mr. Brown nodded approvingly when he saw it. "It's what I'd call — functional," he said. "No thing of beauty, but functional." Father liked to talk that way. Bob was used to it.

"Anyhow, it doesn't wobble," he said proudly. "We'll drill the holes for our wiring later."

"Good." Bob felt warm at his father's praise.

They had the table. They had some track and a few cars. But you wouldn't run them around by hand. Not after you'd seen Mr. Yerkes's pike. You had to have wiring and a power pack. You had to have a locomotive.

A locomotive cost ten dollars. That was the cheapest and the smallest. They would have to buy one in a kit; it was too complicated to make the parts for one by themselves. Some of the other cars they were sure they could make, but not a locomotive. Ten dollars! Why, that was terrific. Good-by to their Christmas money! And if they spent ten dollars for a locomotive, they wouldn't have money for anything else.

Gloom settled over the meeting in the cellar. All at once Skinny said, "We're a club, aren't we? Even if we don't have officers and a constitution and everything."

"Sure."

"Well, then, why don't we take in more members? And have dues? That way we can raise money for what we need."

It was a good idea. The others wondered why *they* hadn't thought of it.

"Who'd we have?"

"We'll have to be careful. We don't want just anyone."

"Bruce McFarlane —" Orphie suggested.

"Yeah, Bruce. He's not much good on mechanics," Bob said importantly, "but he knows how to make other things. . . . He's sort of artistic. He could do the scenery, the mountains and lakes and things."

Bruce was one. "And maybe Clint?" Skinny said slowly.

"I guess so. He's older than us and he likes to boss, but we'll have rules so he can't boss too much."

That was two. They would need more. It was bound to get around at school that they were forming a model railroad club, and they would probably have dozens to choose from.

Almost right away Chip Randolph said he wanted to join. "We'll let you know," Bob said guardedly. Chip had money, plenty of it, and he could always get more. That would be fine for the club's treasury, but they weren't too sure about Chip himself.

They held a meeting about it. "He's sort of — wild," Skinny said.

"Maybe he would ball things up."

"Yes, but if we don't have him he'd probably make a lot

30

of trouble, too. . . . I guess we could keep him in line," Bob said.

They took a vote on it, and decided, gloomily, to have Chip. He would have worked himself into the group anyhow, they thought, and they might as well ask him first.

They got Jan Larssen in, too. The Larssens lived in back of the Browns. They liked Jan. The only trouble with him was that he never had any money. That is, he had it — but he spent it so fast he never had it when he wanted it, or when it was needed.

"I tell you what," Bob said strongly. "We'll warn him that if he doesn't come across with his dues and assessments right off the bat, he's out. That'll get him!"

They finally decided on three more. Peter Daly, who was a good sort; Karl Baumann, steady and plodding, but bright enough; Matt Evans, clever with his hands, although he was always inclined to take a dark view of things.

The other boys seemed to consider it an honor to be asked to join. They agreed to meet twice a week in the Browns' cellar and work on the pike. Between times, each one could work on individual pieces of equipment — whatever best suited him. Bruce would do the scenery.

The main thing to vote on was what kind of railroad they would have. It took them a whole afternoon's discussion, and even then it wasn't settled. Clint was all for a coal-hauling road. Skinny wanted one that specialized in cattle and dairy hauling. Orphie thought it would be fun to have mostly passenger cars and up-to-date engines. Bruce said he didn't care, he would make whatever scenery they needed.

"Why can't we have some of each?" Bob finally asked. "Keep everybody happy. Later on, when we see how things work out, we may decide to go in for one thing more than the other."

"Okay," they said. It was one way of settling it — by leaving the question open for a while.

Bob went into the cold-room to get some apples for the gang. The apples came from their own tree, and always tasted special. He had just bitten into a particularly fine one when Pat came charging down the stairs.

"Bob, Bob, what do you think?"

"I think you've busted into a meeting," Bob said severely.

"It's time you quit anyhow," Pat said, not at all daunted. "Mother says to come up soon because we have to get Mr. Kendall's room ready."

"Mr. Kendall?" Bob echoed, his mind far away. "Why?"

"He's going to live with us, silly," Pat said impatiently. "He's going to be our new boarder. Isn't that wonderful?"

It really was no great surprise. When Mr. Teague had left, Mother had said almost at once that they ought to have someone else come to stay with them. They were such a happy family, she said, and they ought to share themselves with someone who had no family. The minute she met Mr. Kendall and heard that he was lonely and lived in a hotel, and saw how he enjoyed her cooking, it was pretty certain that he would be invited to stay at their house.

"Okay," Bob said cheerfully. "If it's got to be someone, it might as well be Mr. Kendall. When's he coming?"

"Tonight," Pat said. "For supper. He was going to come Monday, but Mother said she was making apple pie and he said why couldn't he come right away? So she said all right. Hurry up — there's a lot to do."

Aunt Meg had called them "the expandable Browns." They were always taking in a person or an animal, or both at once. Now it was going to be Mr. Kendall. Thinking of this, Bob laughed.

"Here we go again!" he said.

CHAPTER 3

Kenny managed to corner Bob in the garden a few days later when Bob was clearing the walk that ran around the house. "I'm going to join the Caboose Club, too," he announced.

Bob gave an inward groan. He had known that there would be no chance to keep news of the formation of the Caboose Club from inquisitive Kenny, who seemed to have antennae on his head when he wanted to know anything. But he *had* thought Kenny might have sense enough to keep out of it. Didn't he know he wasn't wanted?

"You're too young," Bob said shortly. Kenny ought to know that, too.

Kenny pulled petulantly at the muffler his mother had wound around his neck. "That's no reason," he said with a pout.

"Sure it is. A good one." Bob heaved a shovelful of snow and flipped it onto the grass. Some of it fell on Kenny. Any other time he would have let out a howl, but now he just brushed it off. That was some improvement, Bob thought sourly.

"No, it's not a good reason," Kenny continued. He had a one-track mind sometimes. "Listen! If I'm too young now, next year I'll be older but you'll be older too and I'll still be younger than you are . . . so I'll never catch up. I'd never be old enough to join."

"You're right," Bob grinned, in spite of himself.

"Well, you see?" Kenny took him up quickly. "And I want to!"

"Okay, you want to," Bob told him; "but that's not all there is to it. You're too young for now. Wait a couple of years." Anything could happen in that time, he thought. "And then maybe we'll see. *You'd* be older then, as old as we are now, and you'd know what it's all about."

"I'd know what it's all about if you'd tell me," Kenny persisted, like a gnat. "Besides, in a couple of years, when you say I'm old enough, maybe there wouldn't be any Caboose Club any more."

"That's a risk you've got to take," Bob said shortly.

"And another thing," Kenny came closer, "I've got money. I could pay dues. Whatever dues you say. I've got lots of money."

He had, too. That was a temptation. They were going to need plenty of money for the club. But having money wasn't that important. If it meant taking in Kenny, they'd have to find some other way.

"Nothing doing," he said.

"You can't decide by yourself," Kenny told him. (He must have been listening somewhere when they made the rules.) "If you're a club you have to ask the others. I want to join, so *I'll* ask the others — unless you do."

That was true. It wasn't too bad, though, because Bob knew, even before asking, what the other boys would say.

"If we did let him in," Skinny said, at the next meeting, "we'd have to let all the little kids of the neighborhood join. We'd be having a kindergarten. And if they're like Kenny . . ." He held up his hands and rolled his eyes comically.

"Nix on Kenny," the others said swiftly.

Bob knew Kenny better than they did. Hadn't he been coping with him for a year? "We'll have to do something about him," he said glumly. "I got to thinking. Maybe we could make him a sort of apprentice — you know, have him run around to get things we want, and clean up. We could keep him busy and out of our pockets. He could be at the meetings but we wouldn't have to let him work on the railroad."

"Nope," they said, practically with one accord. "That wouldn't do. First thing you know, he'd be in on everything. Kenny's out."

Bob said gloomily, "You don't know Kenny the way I do."

And sure enough, at the very next meeting, there was Kenny. Not right away. But halfway through the evening Bob looked up and saw him coming down the cellar steps.

36

"Hey!" he shouted angrily. "Who said you could come here?"

"I didn't come to the club," Kenny announced. "I came to visit Suzie. And she's getting apples, and she said I could come down with her."

Suzie was instructed to keep Kenny out of the way, but it didn't help much. Next time he came down he said he had come to visit Pat. And the time after that it was Mrs. Brown, of whom he was very fond. After all, the boys couldn't very well tell him to get out, because it was the Browns' house, and not just the club's.

"Well, what *can* we do?" Skinny demanded. "He comes down here and hangs around, and talks, and wants to know what everything is, and picks things up —"

"Don't talk to him," Clint said positively. "Give him the cold shoulder."

But that didn't really work, either. Kenny didn't even notice. And you can't give the cold shoulder to someone who doesn't even notice. After a while they decided they'd just have to put up with him, and by that time Kenny considered himself a member.

The Caboose Club got along fine for a while. Everybody had some Christmas money to spend, and was working on the kit he had bought. Dues were all paid in — even Jan had paid his promptly — and Orphie kept the accounts.

They had decided, by a vote, to make it a railroad that carried mostly freight — but with some passenger service.

37

And it would be an imaginary road, one they invented. Not a real one. That way, they wouldn't have to conform so closely to existing conditions and markings, but would have the fun of making up their own.

The name of the road hadn't been decided on yet. They were having a hard time with that.

"Pooh!" Pat said. "What's hard about it? I could make one up for you in no time at all."

"What, for instance?" Bob tried not to sound doubting.

"Well," Pat played with the end of one of her red braids thoughtfully, "let me see. There are ten of you," she began. Her face brightened. "See, there it is! There are ten of you — why not call your railroad the Big Ten?"

Bob said it over a couple of times. "The Big Ten . . . Not bad! There used to be a Big Four railroad, I think. . . . We could be the Big Ten!"

Pat pressed her chance. "I can letter the name on all the cars and equipment!"

"Well, you can do it upstairs, then," Bob said sternly. "No girls allowed as members."

"Who said I wanted to be a member?" Pat rejoined. "I've got lots more interesting things to do."

In a few weeks a half-dozen cars were finished and they were working, too, on the table layout of track. Matt was good at track, and so was Karl. They teamed up well together.

Mr. Brown came down one evening to help them with

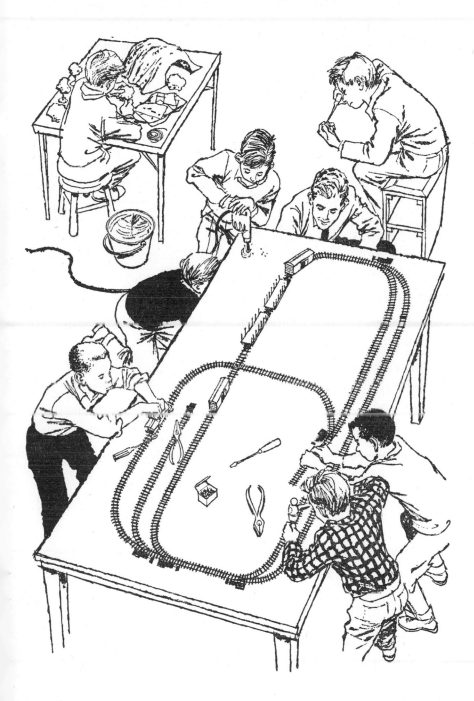

their power pack. Bruce was off in a corner at an old card table, his bucket of soaked newspapers for papier-mâché beside him. He was delicately attaching a bit of sponge to a tree made of wire. It would be painted later. His sister Bonnie had come over to see Pat, and Pat had brought her down.

She was sort of like a boy, Bob thought, with her close-cut dark hair and dungarees, and they didn't mind her too much. She didn't talk a blue streak, either . . . just stood and watched.

Right now she was watching Clint trying to set some tiny screws in a piece of draft gear. Clint was having a bad time of it, either dropping the screws or starting them in crooked.

Bonnie watched him try for the tenth time; then she took it out of his hands, and set the screws deftly. "You're a southpaw, aren't you?" she asked as he snatched the car back.

Clint's face flushed. He mumbled "Thanks," and went on with the assembly. Bonnie didn't seem to notice. She came over to where Bob and Skinny were struggling with some wiring, under Mr. Brown's directions. They didn't want *him* to do it, they wanted to do it themselves.

She bent down and peered under the table to watch them. "Better leave more slack than that," she said, almost at once.

Bruce came to squat beside his sister. "What for?" he demanded. "It'd look a lot neater if we had it lying flat, wouldn't it?"

"Sure it would," she retorted. "And then if you ever wanted to put in another piece of track, or some extra thingummies — like lights or signals — you wouldn't have any power lead wire to spare."

"She means," Skinny said tolerantly, "that you have to have plenty of extra length if you're going to splice on any lead wires."

Clint looked up. "Yeah," he said, "you want to be sure and have plenty of slack in your power lead." That was like Clint.

Mr. Brown looked amused, but said nothing. Bruce was still puzzled. "But why do you need slack for splicing?" he asked.

"Because when you splice wire, you have to cut it back, and take off some of the insulation, and scrape it. So every time you put in a new switch, for instance, you'd lose some more of your wire."

"Well, why are you using different colored wires?" Bruce asked the boys, ignoring his sister's explanation.

Skinny shook his head, as if marveling at Bruce's ignorance. "So we can tell the different circuits apart," he said.

"You didn't think we were trying to decorate the underside of the table, did you?" Clint demanded.

Bruce flushed, and turned away. "I just wanted to know," he said in a low voice.

Skinny said swiftly, "Cheer up! I couldn't make that scenery to save my neck. I guess we're turning into a — a bunch of specialists."

Bob spoke up to cover an embarrassing pause. "I'm not

too sure just how this whole power business works. I mean, what will make the engine run, and everything? I know *what* to do to make it run, but I don't know *why* it does."

Mr. Brown straightened up. "You boys certainly should know the 'why' of what you're doing. Maybe I can explain it to you." He thought for a moment. "You know that electricity can magnetize, don't you? And that a magnet has two poles — the north and the south — that attract each other?"

The boys nodded. "Well, then, in every electric motor there is a magnet. Sometimes it's shaped like a horseshoe. Inside that magnet is an armature — that is the moving part of the motor; and it has several little electromagnets attached to it. The whole thing is placed so that it will rotate inside the two poles of the magnet. . . . To put it simply: when electricity is fed into the armature through a brush, the south pole of the electromagnet that happens to be nearest the north pole of the magnet is pulled toward it."

"And that turns it!" Skinny cried.

"Yes, but not enough. Then the commutator changes the polarity of the armature, and instead of being pulled toward the *north* pole of the magnet, it now runs around toward the *south* pole of the magnet. And meanwhile this same thing is happening to the next little electromagnet, and then to the next —"

"And the whole armature keeps turning!" Bob finished.

"What stops it?" Bruce asked. "Shutting off the current?"

"Right. There are different arrangements that can be

made in the positions of these parts, but the principle is the same. Do you get the general idea now?"

Before they could answer, Suzie came tearing down the stairs and flung herself on her father. "Daddy, Daddy, Rex got in a fight! I heard a terrible noise and I went out, and Rex has his ear 'most torn off, and he has a big wounded in his side!" Her tearful face lifted in the light. "Daddy, do you think he'll *die?*"

Mr. Brown dropped everything, and picked up Suzie. "Of course not. Rex is a good fighter, and he's strong. Let's go and see what we can do."

Suzie, from the haven of her father's shoulder, told the others, "Anyhow, Rex chased that other old dog so far you couldn't see him!"

Pat looked worried. "I'll go and see, too," she said. Bonnie went with her.

Bob waited till they were safely out of earshot. Even so, he first looked around cautiously.

"Say," he said in wonder, "how come Bonnie knows so much about electricity and stuff?"

Bruce said nonchalantly, "Oh, she's a whiz at fixing things. If we have a busted cord, or a fuse out, or the iron goes on the blink, she fixes it. Dad taught her."

"Do you know how, too?" Bob asked. "We could use you."

"Me?" Bruce laughed. "I'm the dumb bunny in our house. . . . But don't tell Bonnie I said so. I never could get on to what it was all about. She took to it like a duck to water."

43

Mother doctored Rex with some salve she had on hand, and washed his sore ear, and Suzie's tear-streaked face took on a beatific smile. But when Mother said Rex could not sleep in Suzie's room that night, and certainly not on the foot of her bed, as he usually did, it brought on the storm again. Bob told her to stop crying and he'd fix a cozy bed for Rex in the cellar. Suzie came down to see that Rex had a cushion and an old piece of carpeting and some fresh paper and a bowl of water. She put some dog candies at his side, and flung her arms around his neck in a great hug.

In the morning, before she had her breakfast, Suzie went down cellar to see how Rex had survived the night. She came up slowly.

"I guess the pixies were at our house last night," she said, her yellow head bobbing excitedly.

"Pixies?" Bob stopped short. He had a sudden feeling that something was wrong. "What do you mean?"

"The — the things are all over the floor," Suzie confessed. "You know, sort of every which way. And some are broken, a little. Pixies like to make trouble," she hastened to say. "Pixies often come, and if there isn't anything for them to eat, they do mischief."

"Pixies, my hat!" Bob exploded. "I bet it was Rex."

"Don't you blame Rex," Suzie blazed. "He's sick — he might have died. It was the pixies, I tell you!"

Bob clattered down the steps. *Something* had made mischief all right, and he had an idea it was Rex's long, hard tail. One big swipe, when he got up and walked around in the night, had done the damage. Bits and pieces of cars and scenery were on the floor; two of the boxcars had been broken, and would have to be done over again. They were both Chip's.

He explained things to the Caboose Club members at school. "I'm sorry. . . . It was sort of my fault, because I should have reminded you to put things away. We had said we'd do that — only in the excitement about Rex, I guess we all forgot."

"You mean my freight cars are broken?" Chip demanded, his lower lip protruding angrily. "You can just fix 'em, then."

"We'll help," Bob said. Chip hated doing things over. He hated cleaning up, too. "But you should have had all your stuff in a box, the way we said we'd do."

"It was your dog that did the damage, so you can buy me new ones."

"We won't have to buy new ones," Bob hastened to say. "Maybe just some parts or so. It's mostly a matter of putting them together again."

"Well, then, you do it," Chip said haughtily. "I'm not going to do a lot of hard work on things just so your dog can have fun knocking them to pieces."

He wasn't at the next club meeting. There was a fine if you didn't come to a meeting without sending word. Bob waited upstairs till half-past seven, then he asked his mother if she would call the house and remind Chip of the date.

45

At half-past eight Mrs. Brown called down that she had tried four times and couldn't get an answer.

"Oh, that sounds like the Randolphs," Jan said, filing on a tiny brake wheel. "This is lodge night for his father and his mother's probably out playing bridge. They're always out. Chip has the house to himself lots of times."

"Well, he isn't there now. So where is he?"

"Maybe he forgot."

Orphie, who took charge of their funds, gave a flashing grin. "We can use his fine!"

They were too busy to think much about it. And then Mr. Kendall came home from an early movie. He looked in to see how they were progressing.

"Did you get held up any when the lights went out?" he inquired genially.

"Lights went out?" Bob echoed. "We didn't have any trouble."

"There must have been a power failure in town, though," Mr. Kendall said, roaming about, looking at their handiwork. "I noticed all the street lights were out in the neighborhood. Guess the repairmen haven't had time to get around to this section yet."

Bob said nothing. He had a sudden sinking feeling. He looked at Orphie, and Orphie looked back at him, without saying a word, either. Just then the wail of a police car siren made them all look up. Maybe the police were hunting for Chip. Once before Chip had gone on a shooting spree and

46

shot out ten street lights. It looked as if he had done it again.

Mr. Kendall was staring from one to the other with a puzzled expression. "What's the matter with all of you?" he asked. "You look sort of green. Must be the light in this cellar."

"Yeah," Bob said with relief. "That's it, I guess."

They didn't want to say out loud that it might have been Chip. They didn't even want to say it to themselves. But there it was, a nasty worry. What had got into him, anyhow — *if* he had done it?

Next morning Chip was on the school bus when Bob and Orphie and Clint and Jan got on. "Hi!" he called out. "That was a swell meeting last night, wasn't it?"

They all gawked at him. Then they got it. He wanted them to say Yes, so that all the other kids in the bus would hear it and think he'd been at the meeting. He wanted an alibi. Bob's face felt stiff.

Clint tossed his head admiringly, as if he thought Chip had a lot of daring. He started to say, "You bet!" but the others cried, almost together, "How do *you* know? You weren't there!"

A swift change came over Chip. He didn't look so cocky and sure of himself. He looked furious enough to strike out at them, and his voice was a snarl. "You're a fine bunch of friends!" he yelled. The words hit like stones.

CHAPTER 4

When Bob woke up, it was snowing heavily. He let out a yip of joy and slid into his clothes. This was a chance for the club to earn some money. Here it was the middle of February, and there hadn't been nearly as many snows as they would have liked. Too many households had able-bodied men or boys in them anyhow. But this snow was deep. . . . People would need help. The first thing to do was to line up the prospects, and then he could notify the boys at school.

He ran down his list. "Mrs. Merkel? Bob Brown speaking. You want your walks shoveled this afternoon after school?" He glanced out of the window happily as he talked. It must have been snowing for most of the night. The evergreens were weighted with snow, the doghouse had a hump of snow on the roof, the lawn was a smooth expanse without a sign of bird bath or wading pool. It looked like plenty of jobs. If only it didn't get *too* heavy.

"Yep, I'll be there. Me and Skinny. Don't give the job to

anyone else. And Mrs. Merkel, if you hear of some other person who wants a shoveling job, be sure to tell us, will you?"

He made a cross beside Mrs. Merkel's name. Now to call Mrs. Hornbloom. And Mrs. Dascomb. And Miss Greer.

"Bob, breakfast's ready!"

"Coming, Mom!" He could get in a few more calls before time to meet the bus. "I can eat a whopper, too," he shouted, racing down the stairs. "I've got a lot of jobs lined up. . . . Whee, pancakes!" He hugged his mother. "Morning, Dad. Morning, Mr. Kendall. Hi, Pat and Suzie. How's Rex?"

"I'm fixing his breakfast," Suzie said importantly. "He has to get strong. But I *think* his ear is better, and he was awful good — he didn't lick the medicine off his side."

Mr. Kendall was already half through his breakfast. "You're a lucky boy to live in this house," he told Bob.

"Sure, I know," Bob said easily, sliding into his place. "But why?"

"I never tasted pancakes like this in my life. And you have them all the time."

"Not all the time," Bob explained. "Only every other week. Unless it's very cold; then maybe we have them three times running."

"Let's hope for a bitter-cold winter," Mr. Kendall said fervently.

"With plenty of snow," Bob put in. "We need the money for shoveling it."

Mr. Kendall helped himself to sirup and made a fancy design on his cakes. "Money's a big problem, isn't it?" he asked in his pleasant voice.

Bob grinned. "You said it! It's all I can think about — sometimes."

"On these shoveling jobs . . ." Mr. Brown said seriously. "No more than half an hour at a time, Bob, and then a rest of five full minutes."

"Yes, sir." It was going to cut into the profits, but he had promised his father before that that's the way he would do it — and make the others do it, too. "The trouble is," he said slowly, "some of the kids don't work as hard as the others."

"You're learning it early."

"I know. And it's not fair. . . . I wonder if Chip will show up?"

"Gramma Curtis said," Suzie put in surprisingly, "that it *was* Chip who shot out the lights."

"How did she know?" Bob wheeled on her.

"Well, when I went to see Gramma Curtis," Suzie said, with a side glance at her mother, "to find out if she had any more kittens —"

"Oh, Suzie, not more kittens!" Mother cried, with a funny expression on her face. Suzie was crazy about animals, kittens especially, and was always bringing home strays. She had had several from Gramma Curtis. It had been hard to persuade her to give then away.

"No, she didn't have any . . . yet," Suzie said wistfully.

"She said it was Buck who saw Chip." Buck was Mrs. Curtis's son. "And he telephoned the police. And they came so fast they found him."

"This is the second time he has done that," Father said. "If he's that kind of boy —"

"Nobody pays much attention to him at home, I guess," Bob said. He didn't mean to stand up for Chip, exactly. . . . But it must have been sort of hard to live in a house where your mother and father were always away and didn't care what you did. "I guess we'll have to keep an eye on him more."

"He's not a very good influence in the club, is he?" Father said.

"He's all right, mostly, in the club," Bob hastened to say. "It's when he *isn't* in it that he gets into trouble."

Mr. Brown and Mr. Kendall exchanged glances. "A good recommendation for the club, I should say," Mr. Kendall said.

Chip wasn't on the bus, and he wasn't at school. Bob notified the boys of the jobs that were promised, and Orphie, who had a telephone list of his own, came up with others. They separated into pairs after school and, armed with shovels and fortified with chocolate bars and crackers, set out for their prospects.

Several houses were next door to each other, and Bob, working swiftly and efficiently, had a chance to keep tabs on some of the members. It was what he had noticed before: a couple of the boys — Jan Larssen and Peter Daly, for instance — kept slacking up. It wasn't that they weren't as strong as the others. But they were always leaning on their shovels and telling stories, or eating, or horsing around. Everybody ought to do his share equally. He began to feel angry and red-faced and was just about to call out sharply when he thought better of it. That was no way to make them work.

"Hey, you two! Get going," he yelled instead. "We've got to get done before supper."

"What am I doing this for, anyhow?" Pete yelled back. "I could be earning the money for myself, instead of for the club. Am I crazy or am I crazy?"

"Sure you could," Bob returned. "But then you wouldn't be a club member."

Skinny said with eagerness, "We're doing it for the treasury."

"Wait till you see that engine we're going to buy," Bob urged. "You'll feel different then. Gosh, at this rate, it won't take us long. I figure," he stopped for a moment and did some mental arithmetic, "I figure at the end of today we ought to have twenty-four dollars! Wow! We can buy quite some stuff for that."

It worked. Jan and Peter got back on the job again. The switch engine was one of their pet projects, and both of them had been arguing for more equipment but had been voted down because of the lean funds.

They didn't talk about Chip until they got together after-

wards at Orphie's house for some hot cocoa. It was safe to talk then. "I bet he's mad as hops at Buck Curtis," Clint said.

"He *would* be," Jan said. "Chip hates to get caught."

"How come Buck saw him?"

"He was having dinner with his Mom, and went out to start his truck so it wouldn't freeze up on him . . . and he just happened to see Chip aim at the light down the street and hit it. So he went in and phoned."

"I wonder what they'll do to Chip," Matt said with a worried air. "He's a sap to try that sort of thing."

"He acts sort of wild . . . sometimes," Skinny said. "I guess he doesn't know what to do with himself."

"Dad says he'll probably have to go to Juvenile Court," Bob offered. "And it depends on the judge, then."

"He'd better not try anything funny again — this was the second time," Clint said.

"If he comes to the next club meeting, what are we going to do?" Peter Daly wanted to know.

"Behave as usual," Bob said stoutly. "And ask him why he was so crazy."

They waited with curiosity and some uneasiness for Chip to make his appearance. He came swaggering in late, but offering no excuse. The boys eyed him, no one wanting to make the first comment.

He tossed his cap into a corner, as usual. "Come on, move over," he said. "Give me some room to work."

"You owe dues for three meetings, and a fine for each

54

one," Orphie told him, consulting his book. "Better get paid up first."

"Sure, sure," Chip said easily. He produced a fat wallet and drew out a bill. "This covers it, and keep the change." Chip always had plenty of money.

"Where were you on snow-shoveling day?" Clint asked.

"In court," Chip said shortly. Suddenly his eyes blazed and his face screwed up in anger. "I hate that Buck Curtis like poison!" he cried in a loud voice. "The nasty old squealer!"

"That's right, blame somebody else," Bob said coldly. "What did you expect him to do if he saw you?"

"What did the judge say?" Skinny asked.

"Oh, the usual yakety-yak," Chip said sullenly. "A big long spiel. He has to talk that way, I guess."

"Sure, if you act that way," Orphie said surprisingly. "Was there a fine?"

"Dad paid it."

"What got into you, anyhow?" Karl demanded.

"I wanted to try out my gun."

"You're not supposed to have a B-B. Where'd you get it?"

Chip's smile was secretive. "Wouldn't you like to know?" he taunted.

"Oh, let's leave him alone," Bob said. "*He* thinks he's a big shot . . . and *we* think he's a sap."

Chip doubled up his fists angrily. Then he thought better of it. He wandered around for a while. Nobody talked to him particularly, not so much because they were cutting him out as because they were absorbed in what they were doing.

Clint and Skinny were working on the power pack. Bruce was painting a hillside. He had cut out his wooden forms for it on the power jig saw at school. Then he had covered them with pieces of screening, and covered the screening with papier-mâché. Later he would glue on the tiny trees. Jan and Matt were placing ballast between some ties. Karl was laying track.

After a while Chip cleared his throat loudly. "I bought some sheetwood and stripwood — on my own. Thought I'd make some buildings. Like those in the book."

He undid a bundle he had pulled from his windbreaker pocket and laid out his supplies. From a small box he produced a tiny combination station — freight and passenger. It was almost complete, and very well done. "We need a station, no matter what kind of layout we decide to have, and this could be it."

Bob came over and inspected it. "It's real neat," he said. "When it gets painted it'll look swell."

Some of the other boys drifted up, one by one. "Yeah, that looks good." They spoke quietly, but Chip seemed happy about their praise.

"I thought I'd go in for buildings," he said hesitantly.

Clint scoffed. "Because they're easier, I guess! I could do that sort of thing with my hands tied behind me . . . you got to be really smart to work on engines and power lines."

"So what?" Chip rejoined. "Stay with your engines and power lines. That leaves the field open for me."

When Mr. Brown came down to help them set up the power pack the air was a little tense, but he seemed not to notice. This was the night they were to try out their locomotive. They would have their first chance to see their handiwork in operation.

Skinny and Clint were the main workers on the pack. While Mr. Brown was explaining to Skinny how the d. p. d. t. (double-pole, double-throw) knife switch worked, Clint made the final connection.

He turned on the current. There was a swift flash, then a hum. Mr. Brown snapped off the switch quickly. "You have a short circuit," he said. Clint looked aghast. "Why didn't you wait till we made sure everything was okay?"

"Gee," Clint said, "I guess I just *couldn't* wait."

Mr. Brown said calmly, "And now you'll *all* have to wait while we fix the short. . . ." He looked around at the circle of disappointed faces. "Does anybody know why Clint had that short?" he asked. They shook their heads.

"Well, then, here's a good place to set you straight. Do you see that screw driver lying across the track? That did it — this time. You have to be watchful and make sure that none of your tools is touching the rails before you turn on the current. But all kinds of things can make a short — careless wiring at one of your extra feeds, for instance. Or failure to put in gaps in the rails near your switches."

"What happens if you don't turn off the current in a hurry?" Bruce asked.

"As you boys have things set up — plenty. You can burn out your rectifier in no time; you can ruin your transformers. In other words," Mr. Brown concluded, "it might be a good idea for you kids to invest in a circuit breaker."

"How much does it cost?" Skinny demanded at once.

Orphie looked it up in the supply book. "Fifty-five cents," he announced lugubriously.

"Well, let's get one," Clint said grandly.

"If you'd been careful, we wouldn't need one," Jan said.

"Yes, but I'm not the only one," Clint said swiftly. "Might as well play safe. Some of you guys can make a mistake, too."

"We can use that fifty-five cents for something else. Everything costs money — if we spend our money on things like this, when all we have to do is to take care —"

"Let's wait a while," Jan said. "We know what makes a short now and what not to do — we'll know better next time."

Matt said anxiously, "What do you think, Mr. Brown?"

He said in a quiet voice: "It's your money, and your decision. . . . But sometimes a layout of money in the beginning saves money in the end."

After he had gone upstairs they put it to a vote, and decided to wait. The expenditure for a second engine had left the treasury pretty depleted. That was what influenced their decision, for the most part, as Bob explained to his father at breakfast next morning. That, and the idea most of them had that they would be more careful, and that shorts would not occur in the future.

"Gosh," Bob said with a gusty sigh, "money sure can disappear when you're buying stuff for a model railroad!"

"I've noticed that it has a way of doing that even in running a house," Mother put in. "More muffins, Mr. Kendall?"

"I wish you'd call me Wayne," Mr. Kendall begged, reaching for one. "Then I'd feel more as if I belonged in the family."

"All right, Wayne," Mother said at once, with her bubbly laugh. "Everybody in the *family* gets three."

"Money seems to be plaguing you guys," Mr. Kendall said, with a smile in Bob's direction. "How about earning some extra?"

"How?" Bob asked eagerly. "It's not so easy to earn money without working papers . . . and keeping up with school and everything."

"Well, I'm having to do a lot of paper work at home this winter. I'm tossing papers into the wastebasket at a great rate, I notice," Mr. Kendall said, "and I thought the other day it's a shame to have my nice room look so messy. So if you could keep an eye on that basket and empty it right along —"

"Why, sure," Bob agreed. "But I —" He broke off, wondering if he ought to say it. It *was* a good chance to earn extra money, and it was all for the club.

He felt his mother's eyes on him. "Go on, Bob," she said firmly, "and tell Mr. Kendall that that's part of your regular household chores and you can't take money for that."

He mumbled, his eyes down, "Yeah, I was just going to." He might have known he wouldn't get away with anything like that, not with Mother! He wondered why he had even hesitated.

Mr. Kendall said easily: "I know how those things are. Well, here's another idea: Considering that storm we had the other day, you might give my windows a wash, inside and out — that is, if you have one of those long-handled mops I see people using —"

"That, too," Mother said, even more firmly, "is part of the household routine. Bob, didn't you do Mr. Kendall's room when you did the rest of the second floor?"

This was a bad morning. "I'm sorry," he managed, between bites of muffin. "I was sort of rushed . . . and I went to empty the pail . . . And then I forgot to go back."

Mr. Kendall looked in admiration at Mother and with sympathy at Bob. "Okay, that's out. . . . Still, there are lots of things I could have a chap like you do for me. I'll think of something," he said cheerfully. "I don't suppose you could use a little loan?"

Bob couldn't help grinning at him. "I could use it," he said, "but I don't think I would dare take it!"

It was nice of Mr. Kendall to want to help out. The chances that had loomed up had gone glimmering — but Mother was right. Maybe Mr. Kendall would come across with another idea, and maybe not. Bob couldn't count on it. He'd just have to find some other way of making money.

CHAPTER 5

Skinny was excited. "You know what? Pop had to see Mr. Yerkes last night on business, and he took me along. I got to telling Mr. Yerkes what a tough time we were having getting enough money for the equipment we wanted to buy, and he gave me a swell idea."

"Spill it," Bob said, and the others echoed him.

"Well, Mr. Yerkes said" — Skinny leaned across the table and his eyes were glittering — "he said, Why didn't we hunt through our attics or closets for old trains? There's a market for them. People collect old stuff — can you beat it? Why, the minute he said it I remembered that old train set I had! It was a big one, too, because my Pop and my Grandpop were always giving me more cars or engines or track. I rushed home and asked Mom where it was" — he leaned back and his face was funny — "and she said, my goodness, she'd given that away long ago, when she thought I had outgrown it!"

"Well, you had," Orphie said.

"Yeah, but now I could have used it!" he said in an aggrieved voice.

"Golly," Bob was mournful, too. "We had a set, but I gave mine to Mom's nursery school kids to play with . . . and there's not much left. What there is wouldn't bring a cent, and we've already used the transformer."

The air brightened a little when Karl and Pete said they had had train sets and thought they were still intact. "And we can ask around among our friends and see what we can dig up," Jan said helpfully. "If everybody asks, say, ten people, we ought to dig up quite a lot."

As it turned out, they didn't get much. Most of the boys who had sets didn't want to part with them, and those that were offered were in a rather battered condition. The worst blow fell when they took what they had collected to show to Mr. Yerkes.

Bob saw him hide a smile, which he managed to turn into a little cough. His voice was kind, though. "I suppose 'old' is a comparative term," he said. Some of the boys looked puzzled, but Bob knew right away when he meant. "Maybe 'old' to you fellows is just a few years back . . . because you haven't lived very long yet. But to oldsters like myself, 'old' means — in *our* youth, or even beyond that. We call trains such as this 'modern.' What I meant was the kind of trains your dads had, or even your grand-dads. Pieces of equipment from that long ago are really valuable."

"We'll ask our fathers, then," Jan said, after a gloomy silence. "And the fathers of our friends."

"A good idea," Mr. Yerkes said, heartily. "Here's wishing you luck! And if you find any, don't do anything to them. If they've still got the original paint job, leave it on."

Luck wasn't with them. Those families who had attics in their houses seemed to have them filled with anything and everything except old trains. And those who lived in apartments — well, there just wasn't room in an apartment, as anyone knew, to keep stuff that you weren't using. All they managed to turn up were a few cars and a funny little steam engine that Steve Malden's father had kept because he thought Steve might want them someday. But in their search they did manage to find a few sets from which they could take the rheostats for their own use. . . . And that was something, as they told each other.

"Look!" Skinny said, one day. "We're dopes! We're just asking around among the fellows we know. . . . Why don't we put an ad in the school paper?"

"It would cost money," Orphie reminded him.

"Sure, I know," Skinny said impatiently, "but sometimes you have to spend money to *make* money. My pop said so." He looked around the little group. "We could put an ad in the paper, or we could put a notice on the bulletin board —"

"That's the ticket!" Bob said excitedly. "That would be free, and I'll get Pat to letter it for us!"

"Okay, let's do it," they agreed. "We'll ask Mr. Nairn for permission, and you work on Pat awhile."

"She'll do it," Bob said with assurance. "All she wants is

an excuse to use those lettering pens, and she's getting good, too."

To their amazement and joy, the announcement on the bulletin board did bring a few good items. At least, they *hoped* they were good. The kids at school thought of it as something of a treasure hunt, and for several days they kept bringing equipment in all stages of disrepair or of a kind that the boys hadn't seen before. Orphie was very cautious. "How do we know what it's worth?" he demanded. "If we pay them money for it, and then we find out it isn't worth anything —"

"We'll ask Mr. Yerkes," Bob decided suddenly. "We'll get a list of men he knows who are looking for old equipment, and then we'll get a list of prices from that man in the Woodcrest store — he's a nice guy and he'll help us out."

The idea worked well. Mr. Yerkes was glad to supply the names of several men who, he knew, were looking for pieces to add to their collections, and they sold several items to them for a pleasant sum. And the rest they disposed of through the Woodcrest dealer in model railroad equipment. What's more, he promised to help them out whenever they had collected more.

That sounded very nice, and they were hopeful for a while. But then it seemed that they had turned up all the old equipment there was in the neighborhood; and by that time, several of the men who might have given them other pieces had decided that they might start a collection themselves.

Still, the treasury, in spite of what Orphie had had to pay out, had a nice balance, and they all felt that it had been time well spent. Now they had some money in reserve, and they were going to need it. It was amazing how quickly you could spend money in a hobby shop! They had to take votes on what they would buy next, and what they would put off to another time. They had had to invest in circuit-breakers, after all. In spite of their good resolutions, they had had one short circuit after another.

Most of the boys, of course, were buying supplies or model kits out of their own money, and working on them at the Caboose Club meetings and at home. The club funds were to go for equipment that was to be shared by all of them.

Even so, it was getting complicated. Some of the equipment was the club's, some of it belonged to the individual boys. How to keep it apart, and without bringing on quarrels, was a problem.

Mr. Kendall solved it. "Everybody ought to mark his own," he said one night at dinner.

Pat nearly choked on a mouthful of cake. "Let me!" she cried. "Let me mark it! I'll invent a special mark for each member, or I'll print his whole name, or his initials, whatever you decide!"

Bob looked at her with amusement. "Okay, you're elected." Then the sound of his own words horrified him. "I mean, not elected to the club, you understand — just to do the lettering."

"Who wants to belong to your old club?" she flared, her red braids bobbing.

"And I'll build a set of shelves," Mr. Kendall was saying with relish, "and make compartments, so each of you can put your gear in your own compartment."

Pat cried eagerly, "And I'll letter each member's name on the compartments! What a chance!"

"What a sister!" Bob said. Pat looked at him questioningly, but he really seemed to mean something nice.

"By the way," Mr. Kendall said, "my car needs a wash. Think you could manage it, along with all your other duties?"

"You bet!"

"I pay a dollar and a half for a wash downtown," Mr. Kendall began.

"I'll do it for a dollar," Bob assured him eagerly. "And wipe out the inside, too."

"Sold. I'll pay you to shine my shoes, too."

Car washing! That would be a good source of income. Bob was deciding to suggest it to the other club members when Suzie came out of the barn. She had Doctor Quack on a long braided red cord and was taking him for an airing. Doctor Quack had grown alarmingly; he seemed almost as tall as Suzie, but she was able to manage him nicely. While Bob scrubbed and polished the car, Suzie got a small chair from the discarded nursery school furnishings and heaved Doctor Quack up on it.

"What's the idea?" Bob inquired good-naturedly. Doctor Quack had promptly got down again.

"I'm teaching him to sit on a chair," Suzie said gravely.

Bob suppressed a guffaw. After all, with Suzie, you never could tell. She had a way with animals. "Be sure you teach him how to use a knife and fork and napkin, too," he urged.

"Maybe I will," Suzie answered. And at that Bob *did* laugh.

Everything was going fine with the club. Kenny wasn't too much of a nuisance — they had had to sit on him a couple of times, but now he knew his place. And Bonnie had continued to pop in on occasions, but she had been shown her place, too. She had helped out with the wiring several times when Mr. Brown couldn't be there — and he had said she had the right ideas.

Not that they told her so. Girls were apt to get swell-headed if you told them things like that.

Then they had trouble. It was Chip's fault. In the night, after their last meeting, Bob heard a funny dull thud. It wasn't Rex: Rex had long since recovered and returned to Suzie's bedroom. . . . Then there was a queer coal-gas smell. It didn't last long, and Bob went back to sleep.

In the morning, when he went down, he discovered what had happened. There had been a small explosion of coal gas in the flue. Soot was over everything in the cellar! Everything! He stood in the middle of the floor and felt like holding his head. All their work — the tiny cars and engines, the

track and loose parts, the scenery Bruce was making — all
had a film of soot on it.

He had to tell the members about it at school. They were
indignant. "It was your fault!" they shouted at Chip. "You
were the last one up, and it was your turn to have covered
everything with the oilcloth!"

Chip's face was flushed. "You needn't try to blame it all
on me!" he shouted back. "Why didn't you cover your own
stuff?"

"Don't try to crawfish out of it!" Matt told him angrily.
"We agreed to take turns, and it was your turn."

"I forgot," he muttered sullenly. "And anyhow, *my* stuff's
ruined, too."

"It's not ruined," Bob said swiftly. "But it's got to be
cleaned, every bit of it."

"It'll take us weeks!" they moaned.

And then Clint pointed his finger at Chip. "You've got to
do the cleaning!"

Chip stood with his feet apart, glaring defiantly at them.
"Well, I won't."

"You've got to clean more than the rest of us," Pete said,
"because it was your fault."

"Why should I? I'll buy new equipment — I've got the
money!"

"Money!" they taunted. "That's not the whole thing. We
want the cars and the stuff we made . . . and they can be
cleaned. We'll do part of it, but you've got to do most of it."

"I won't, I tell you. I'll get out of the club."

"Okay, get out. . . . But not before you clean up your share of the mess."

Skinny said quietly, "Starting tonight."

They had ganged up on him, Chip knew. And there was no getting out of it. They all hated the job, though, scrubbing and dunking and polishing and wiping . . . but, miraculously, some damp cloths and cleaning fluid and elbow grease were getting results. It would take them this whole evening and another one to get their gear in shape again.

The real loss was some of the scenery, but Bruce was almost happy about that. "I wasn't so sold on some of that stuff I did, anyhow," he said. "I'll work on some pieces at home, and I've got different ideas by now. I can make it better. This was only practice."

Just the same, there was a queer feeling in the air that evening. Uncle Bill noticed it when he came down for a visit. He looked around the group. "What's the matter?" he inquired. "You look like a bunch of galley slaves."

"We're clearing up a mess." Bob explained what had happened, careful not to say anything about Chip.

"*Umm,*" Uncle Bill said. "There's trouble on a real railroad every now and then, too." He dug in his pocket. "Speaking of a real railroad, I brought you kids something I think you can use."

Bob tried to sound lighthearted. "A diesel?"

"No, a timetable."

They had looked up expectantly when Uncle Bill said he had brought something, but now their faces fell. Anybody could get a timetable.

"Uh, thanks," Bob managed. "But we've all got time-tables around the house."

"I mean the real thing," Uncle Bill persisted. "Not the kind for passenger trains alone. The kind the dispatcher uses. . . . Every train, passenger and freight, marked out. Look here, I'll show you how it's arranged."

They crowded around the table, their cleaning jobs forgotten. This was something else again!

"We could work out one for our pike!" Bob cried.

"Sure thing!"

"I'll do it," Chip announced firmly. "That's the kind of thing I'd like to do."

"I thought you said you were going to leave —" Clint began. Karl shoved an elbow in his ribs — hard — and he stopped. Uncle Bill hadn't seemed to notice anything.

They listened respectfully to what Uncle Bill told them. After all, he *knew* — he was connected with a real railroad. . . . He explained how precisely things had to be worked out. You had to know where every train was at a given moment, allow for passing, for the removal of certain cars from a train, for the making up of a longer or shorter train, for taking on or discharging freight, and also you had to maintain schedules for passenger service. The sheet before them was complicated — and fascinating.

Mr. Yerkes had said that quite a few model railroaders enjoyed working out a similar kind of schedule for their pikes. Each of them would have liked a try at it himself, but Chip had snagged the job now. Maybe it was just as well. Chip was pretty good at math, and it would keep him busy — after he had done the rest of his cleaning.

He set to work with a will, now that he foresaw an end to the loathesome task. For the rest of the evening, and at home, he spent hours over the timetable for the pike. They had two engines now — a new little Mantua shifter, which they had bought with the money from the sale of old trains and cars, and the regular diesel. Also a passing siding and one crossing. And a good loop of track besides. It wasn't very much, but it was enough to make some interesting combinations. And Chip told them he would work out as complicated a time-table as possible.

They caught his enthusiasm. "Then we can each have a turn at running it," they said.

The following week Chip came with his schedule neatly typed. It looked interesting. Skinny, when they drew lots, got first chance at manipulating the switchboard. The Browns' electric kitchen clock was plugged in and hung from an overhead pipe facing him. One second on the clock represented one minute on the timetable; one minute on the clock was one hour on the timetable.

"Now you follow exactly what I've got!" Chip said sternly, and Skinny said humbly that he would.

73

The rest of them crowded around. Skinny, with an anxious eye on the clock, pressed the first button. The freight train started to move.

Around the track. Three times around, and then a stop at the station. The engine switcher appeared and uncoupled three freight cars and herded them onto the passing track, after which it returned to engage two other cars. Now both trains started up. The freight train continued around the track; the switcher took its cars halfway around the second loop and over to the crossing.

Then it happened. The switcher, with its following cars, plowed into the rear end of the freight train.

"Cut the switch!" Orphie yelled. Skinny had already done so.

Bob's caboose had been on the end of the train. The engine had mangled its grab-irons and rear platform. The ladder was twisted, the marker lights were bent. He would have to buy new parts and do over some of the work, re-attaching the delicate brake-wheel, the tiny lamps, the ladder. And the couplers! They were twisted out of shape. The couplers had caused him a lot of trouble in the first place.

"Look what you've done, you goop!" Chip cried angrily. "Why didn't you follow my timetable?"

"I did!" Skinny retorted. "I was right on the dot. You made a mistake in your figuring."

"I did?" Chip gave a rough laugh. "That's right, blame somebody else. You should have read it over first, learned it

74

by heart. And anyhow, couldn't you *see* what you were doing?"

"I tell you I did follow it," Skinny yelled. "Just the way you had it. You've got things too close . . . you didn't allow enough time . . ." He broke off and turned a stricken face to Bob. "Gosh, Bob, I'm sorry about your caboose. I wouldn't have hit it for anything. I guess I was watching the clock just then. I'll help you fix it —"

Bob swallowed hard. "I — I guess real railroads have wrecks now and then. It's a good thing it wasn't a passenger car full of passengers."

"Something went wrong, that's sure," Jan said, giving Bob's shoulder a friendly pat. "And it looks like —"

"Now, listen, don't try to tie it on me," Chip cried furiously. "I spent hours on that schedule, and just because Skinny balled it up by being careless —"

Bob pulled himself together. They would end in a free-for-all, first thing you knew. Somebody *was* to blame, but who? Trains didn't wreck themselves.

He said, above the clamor of voices, "Let's quit beefing and go at it from the beginning." Skinny's downcast face and Chip's belligerent attitude spurred him on. "Now we'll go over this thing again; but we'll only run one train at a time, and we'll time each one as accurately as we can. Maybe that way we can discover what was wrong, and take a vote on it."

While he talked, his fingers lingered over the banged-up

75

caboose. He had a special feeling for it. It had been his first job, and even now he could remember the excitement and satisfaction he had felt working on it. None of the other things he had done had meant quite as much to him as that caboose — which had opened up a whole new field of interest.

They started at the beginning of the schedule, checking each time with the clock. Everything went fine until 10:24. Then — Orphie let out a shout at what he had spotted and they all saw it at once — there was a conflict on the timetable. The switcher had only two minutes' clearance, instead of four, and that's why it had plowed into the rear of the train.

"See!" Jan said triumphantly. "That was the reason!"

Chip glowered at him.

Bob said hastily, "Ready for the vote?"

They spoke up bravely, in spite of Chip's threatening attitude. Skinny was cleared; it *had* been Chip's fault.

In a fury, Chip stalked out. Nobody said anything, but they felt relieved, somehow. In less than ten minutes he was back. He flung a five-dollar bill on the table. "Here!" he shouted. "That'll pay for everything."

"Where'd you get it?" Clint demanded.

"Where do you think? From my father." He gathered up his gear in a sweeping gesture, piled it into a piece of oilcloth. "Now we're square, and I'm getting out of here. I don't want to belong to such a crummy club anyhow!"

76

Orphie giggled a little. "Bet you didn't know that 'crummy' is just another word for caboose," he said.

"Not the way I meant it!" Chip sneered.

They were speechless. It left a bad taste in their mouths. But what could you say? Nobody was going to force him to stay on if that's the way he felt about them.

Halfway up the steps Chip collided with Uncle Bill.

"Gangway!" Uncle Bill shouted. "Oh, excuse — I thought I had a clear track!" He gave Chip a friendly shove. "Listen, you kids — come on down, Chip, you'll want to hear this."

There was no time to tell Uncle Bill what they had just been through. Chip remained standing on the cellar steps, hidden from them.

Uncle Bill came into the circle of light. He looked excited. "I've got a whopping piece of news for you. Maybe it's too big for you to swing, but I thought you'd like to know about it anyhow."

"What?" It was sort of hard to sound interested.

Uncle Bill leaned forward. "It's a real caboose — from a real railroad!" he cried. "They're going to sell it off. The railroad does that with old or surplus equipment every now and then — when they're changing over from wood to metal cars, for instance — and I just heard about it. I found out how much you could get it for, and how much it would cost to transport it, too."

The same thought leaped to all their minds. A clubhouse! A real caboose for the Caboose Club!

"Oh boy — Oh boyoboy!" They began leaping about like dervishes, a thousand ideas crowding each other. This was something they wouldn't have dared dream up. But here was Uncle Bill as real as real — telling them it *could* happen.

"And if you're wondering where you could put it" — Uncle Bill burbled happily — "why, Bob's father says you can set it in the back garden here, at right angles to the barn. What do you say?"

CHAPTER 6

Everybody talked at once.

"We can have it for our club meetings!"

"And use it for our workroom — one end of it, anyhow."

"And we can set up our pike in it!"

"Boy, I'll bet no other bunch of kids has a real caboose for a clubhouse!"

"We haven't got it yet!"

"Well, we will!"

Orphie said, above the others, "How much would it cost?"

Uncle Bill answered readily, "A hundred for the caboose itself, and a hundred to have it brought here."

You could have heard an HO coupling drop in the silence that fell. It beat on their ears. Two hundred dollars! It might as well be the United States national debt! Where in the world would a club like theirs get two hundred dollars?

"And, of course, there would be the cinder-block piers to set it on — you can't just set it on the ground — and you ought to have siding to cover the open area between the piers," Uncle Bill added. Apparently he didn't realize how their hopes had taken a nose-dive. Two hundred dollars!

Matt gave a big sigh. "Well, it would have been nice —"

"*Would* have been?" Bob took him up. "We haven't even begun to talk about it yet."

"What's the use?" Matt argued gloomily. "We could talk about buying the Jersey Central, too. Or the Empire State Building."

"I don't think we need to worry too much about the money," Chip's voice fell strangely on their ears.

Clint looked over his shoulder. "Oh, you back?" he asked sarcastically. Chip ignored him, and the others said nothing.

Chip heaved his untidy package of gear onto the table and said directly to Orphie, "How much have we earned so far?"

They all turned to Orphie at that. It *would* be a good idea to know how much they had earned. Orphie pulled out his little black notebook, considerably worn by now. He moistened the stub of a pencil and added columns of figures, while they stood there, impatiently.

"A hundred and eighty-four dollars," Orphie announced in an awed voice. He didn't seem to believe it himself, and ran swiftly over the last column of figures again.

"See?" Chip said triumphantly. "That's practically two hundred as it is!"

"Yeah," Matt said swiftly, "but I'll bet we've *spent* a hundred and eighty of it!"

"Just about," Orphie agreed. "A hundred and fifty-two, thirty-three."

With $31.67 in the treasury, how could you swing a two-hundred-dollar deal? It looked just about as impossible now as it had before.

"We did it once . . . !" Jan offered.

"But that was because we had lots of snow-shoveling jobs, and there was the sale of that second hand railroad equipment," Matt said quickly.

"And spring's here, and we can't count on any more snow shoveling," Karl said soberly. "And we've collected all the secondhand stuff there is in the neighborhood."

Bob said stoutly, "But we could work as a team at other things."

"Such as what?"

"Well — taking care of lawns and gardens" — heavy groans met his suggestion — "and washing cars, and putting up screens, and things like that."

"Like clearing out cellars, I guess," Clint said with a sneer.

"Yep, that would bring in money, too," Bob answered.

Nobody was very cheerful about the chances for earning money. Especially not a sum like two hundred dollars. Most of them had to do those things at their own homes, as Matt pointed out, for little or no pay. They were *expected* to do chores like that. And other homes nearby had fathers and sons of their own to do the work.

Bob was not to be downed. He said, "I know *I* found a lot of jobs for myself last summer — Gramma Curtis gave me plenty, and I got work at the Aldens' and the Hatches'. . . . I could have had plenty of other places if I'd had the time. If we really canvassed the town, I'll bet we could come up with enough jobs for all of us."

"Make it a motion and I'll second it," Chip said surprisingly.

Bob looked him in the eye. "Are you back in?"

Chip said arrogantly, "I never left, did I? You don't think you can toss me out now, when there's the chance of getting a real caboose!"

The motion went through, while Uncle Bill stood by silently. Nobody was too keen about the idea of all that extra work. . . . but they knew it had to be done. If they teamed up and fell to, it might not have to last too long. Anyhow, why think about work all the time? Why not think about the fun? A caboose of their own! It was still hard to believe.

They plied Uncle Bill with questions.

"How big is it?"

"Thirty by eight — roughly."

"Wow! That's as big as a little house! What's it like inside?"

"Do you have a piece of paper?" Karl tore a sheet off a pad, and Uncle Bill bent down and made a quick sketch. "This is just a rough drawing," he said.

Most of them had a hazy idea of what the interior was like, but now Uncle Bill was making it specific. He drew in two oblongs at one end of the caboose, across from each other, then two more. "This is a bunk — and so is this," he said, "and these are lockers." Toward the center he indicated steps. "This is where you go up to the cupola."

"Boy! A lookout!" Jan cried.

"That's where the brakeman goes to keep a watch," Orphie said quietly. He knew more about railroads than any of the others, of course.

"Down at this end," said Uncle Bill, sketching rapidly, "is the water cooler. . . . Here's the sink. . . . Here's the stove."

"A stove!" Bob cried in excitement. "Sure, we'd need a stove for the winter! Does that come with it?"

"Could be," Uncle Bill said, grinning. "In any case, you can pick one up at an auction before next winter."

Pete wanted to know, "Does the caboose come just as it is?"

"Not exactly. All the metal underneath — the journal box and brake mechanism, the bolsters and trucks — gets stripped and sold for scrap. The wheels, too, of course. That's why you'd have to put it on piers."

"That would cost money, too," Orphie said soberly.

"Everything costs money," Matt said on a lugubrious note.

"Yes, but think what we'd be getting!" Bob cried, his

84

voice full of excitement. "A clubhouse of our very own! . . . The kind of place nobody else would have! . . . And room to work in, and have railroad shows, and space to keep all our truck in!" He turned to his uncle. "Do you think we could do it, Uncle Bill?"

Uncle Bill said quietly, "If you want a thing hard enough, there's generally a way to get it."

"Well, we *want* it enough, don't we, fellas?" Bob asked the group.

"Sure! Sure! You bet!" the answers came back strongly.

"The big problem," Bob said, his feet apart, his head bent in thought, "is how to have the caboose held until we can raise the money. Because raising the money would take time — a lot of time."

"Not too much, I hope," Uncle Bill said. "Because if you don't buy the caboose, somebody else may."

Their faces fell. They couldn't possibly raise that amount of money quickly. Maybe they'd have to give up their dream, after all.

"However —" Uncle Bill said slowly — he drew out a pipe and lit it, and puffed once or twice — "However . . . I think you could manage to borrow the money."

"Not at a bank," Bob said. "No bank would take us on."

"No, not at a bank. A bank would have to demand collateral — something to prove you could pay, and if you didn't, that they could take over — and you don't have that. So you would have to go to people who know you well enough to believe in you, and who would have faith that you would pay up — in time."

"You mean — our parents?" Bob asked, feeling surprised somehow — he didn't know why.

"Who else?" Uncle Bill beamed at him. "You might even include uncles."

"How would we go about it?" Orphie asked.

"Let's call down Bob's father first. . . ."

"Here he comes now!" Bob said, recognizing a familiar step. "And Mr. Kendall, too!"

The two men appeared in the doorway. "Do we hear our names being spoken?" Mr. Kendall asked genially.

"Not in vain, we hope," Uncle Bill said.

But Father said, "I've been busy answering the phone about you kids. Have you any idea what time it is? All your parents seem to think you're lost, strayed or stolen . . . but I told them you were busy hashing over something. Pretty exciting, isn't it?"

"Gosh, we can't believe it!" Bruce said.

"I think you'd better scoot, in a couple of minutes, though — just to keep them from getting gray hair."

"I bet *my* parents didn't call," Chip said, with something of a swagger.

Mr. Brown said quietly, "No, Chip. . . . Not yet."

"They won't, either."

It was hard to tell how he meant it to sound. But the rest

of them knew he was right. Chip's parents never seemed to care where he was or how long he stayed. Maybe that was why he acted so queer sometimes.

Uncle Bill gave a briefing to Bob's father and Mr. Kendall. There wasn't time to talk it all over — not tonight. But Mr. Kendall came up with an idea right away. "You can be thinking about this meanwhile, and asking your parents if they'd be willing to go along with it," he said.

The idea was, he explained, to have a sort of "banking group." The bankers would be the parents, with Uncle Bill and himself.

"I bet Mr. Teague would want to be in on it, too," Bob said with conviction. "After all, he started the whole business, giving me that caboose kit."

"Let that be a lesson to him!" Mr. Kendall laughed. "Well, my idea is, to borrow the money in regular form — I'll draw up an agreement for you, if you like — and with a definite promise to pay within a certain time. And then you can make a down payment on the caboose —"

"I'll see about arranging that," Uncle Bill said promptly.

"And then go about a regular campaign to raise the money within the time you've set," Mr. Kendall went on. "That way you have an aim and a purpose. *And* you have the caboose safely tied up in your back yard meanwhile."

It sounded wonderful. And possible. They put it to a quick vote and everybody was agreed.

"Now scoot!" Father said. "Before I get irate parents on my trail. We'll work out the details in the next couple of days."

Something had to suffer in those next few days . . . and it was school work. After all, you didn't have a chance like this more than once in a lifetime. They knew they could make up the school work when it was all really settled, and they were sure the caboose would be theirs. Their teachers seemed to understand, once they knew what was in the wind, and as for the rest of the school — they were so green-eyed it wasn't funny.

After the fathers had met, and had agreed to lend the money, Bob went to see Gramma Curtis. She had been so helpful last summer, and had been a good friend ever since they moved into the district near her farm home.

"Anything you want done — anything at all, Gramma Curtis," Bob said eagerly, "that you think I could do, why, you let me know about it. We've got to raise money and we're willing to do all kinds of jobs. Tell your friends, too, will you? You have lots of friends."

Gramma Curtis looked up from rolling cookies. "I hope so, Bob," she said. "If you live as long as I have lived, and haven't friends to show for it, it's a pretty poor life." She went over to the oven and pulled out a sheet of finished cakes, brown and cinnamony. "Help yourself — if you like them hot."

"How many?" Bob asked with a grin.

"One for you, one for every day of the week, and six for Suzie."

"That about finishes the sheet," Bob commented, helping himself willingly enough.

"More coming up," Gramma said. "A hundred dollars for the caboose, you said. That's reasonable. And another hundred for trucking. *That's* high."

Bob sighed gustily. "Don't we know it? But Uncle Bill said that's what they charge."

"It's a regular rate, I'll admit," Gramma said. There was a little frown between her brows. "What I meant was, it's awfully high for you boys."

"We'll just have to work harder, I guess," Bob said, stuffing one of the smaller cookies into his mouth. *"Umm,* these are swell, Gramma Curtis! Even better — I mean, almost as good as Mom's."

She smiled at him. "That's right. Nothing could be *better* than your mother's cookies. . . . Look here, Bob, why don't you hold off a bit with the trucking? I could ask my son about rates, or if he knows where you can get a cheaper price. I'm not promising anything —"

Bob gave an impulsive whoop, then clapped a hand over his mouth. "I knew you'd help!" he cried happily. "You let me know as soon as you can, will you? We've *got* to get the caboose trucked to our place — but if we can save even a couple of dollars it would help."

Gramma telephoned that very evening. Buck had heard

the story, she said, and was so impressed with the idea of the club having a real caboose that he had offered to do the trucking himself for much less. "He's never trucked a caboose before, but he can rent a platform truck and he thinks it would be an experience," she told him. He heard her chuckle over the phone. "That Buck!"

Bob was voluble in his thanks. He called his Uncle Bill at once to tell him to go no further with the other trucker who had "almost" been engaged. "We can use that extra money for the cinder blocks and the cement," he said with a businesslike air. "Now we can scout around and see if we can buy some wooden siding cheap."

"Good luck, scout," Uncle Bill said heartily.

The cinder block piers, of course, had to be set in place before the caboose arrived. That would need a committee of fathers to superintend the work — and do some of it! — so it would be done right. Bob alerted the club members, and they set two possible dates. When they got together at school they would decide on the day that turned out to be convenient for most fathers.

At noon recess they took a roll count. Everybody's father could come on the following Saturday except Chip's.

"Why not?" Bob asked.

"Because he can't," Chip said defiantly. "That's his day for golf." His face was flushed, he kept shoving his fists deep into his pockets. "He said there'd be enough around anyhow, he wouldn't be needed."

That was the second time Mr. Randolph hadn't come. He had failed to put in an appearance the night the fathers met to form the banking group. That, Chip said, had been his father's lodge night and he wouldn't miss it for anything.

Suddenly Bob felt a wave of pity roll over him. Chip was acting surly because he was hurt. He knew how *he* would feel if his father had failed him. . . . But that couldn't happen! His father had never failed him. It must be awful not to be able to count on your father. And to have to stand up and tell other guys so.

He said gruffly, "Oh, we'll make out, Chip."

CHAPTER 7

Mr. Teague rolled up his sleeves. His broad heavy face was lit with a grin. "I'm glad you called me in on this, Bob. I'd have felt insulted if I had been left out. Who's my hod-carrier?"

"Kenny," Pete said quickly. Kenny, of course, had come over as soon as the men arrived, demanding to be in on things and asking far too many questions. "Hey, Kenny, come on and get busy!"

"What's a hod-carrier?" Kenny asked now.

"Somebody who carries stuff for the bricklayer," Pete said. "Don't you know *anything*? Mr. Teague will tell you what to do. . . . And see that you do it, or you're out on your ear."

"Oh, Kenny and I will get along all right," Mr. Teague said, with unusual geniality for him. But then, he had certainly become a changed man since he had gone back to his wife. "Is everybody here?"

"Everybody except Mr. Randolph," Skinny said. "And *he's* playing golf."

92

Some of the fathers were mixing mortar; others were lining up the places for the six piers; others were toting cinder blocks from the pile near the barn, and all the boys were helping.

"Looks like we'd get done in record time," Mr. Sparks offered.

"In spite of Mr. Randolph taking the day off," Matt's father said.

"Who does he think he is?" Mr. Larssen demanded, shifting his pipe from one side of his mouth to the other. "All the other fathers took this on . . . why couldn't he?"

"It's the second time he's ditched us," Pete's father said grimly. "But I must say, I didn't really expect much cooperation."

"Well, I did," Mr. Snow said. "The least he could do after passing up being one of the 'banking group' was to take on his share here."

"Golf's more important, apparently."

Chip, standing behind them with an armload of blocks, suddenly let them fall. "You don't know what you're talking about!" he said rudely. His face was an angry red. "If my father wants to play golf, that's his business. And you needn't keep talking about him, either!"

"Sorry, Chip." Several men spoke at once. "We missed him, that's all, and we think he's missing something, too."

"You've got plenty of people here — you don't need him," Chip said defensively.

93

"Look what you did!" Jan shouted, running up. "Two of the blocks are busted!"

"So what?" Chip demanded, still furious. "I'll pay for 'em."

"Well, watch what you're doing," Jan said with a stern air. "We only bought what we figured we'd need, plus a few extra, and if you — or anybody else — busts 'em, we're out of luck. We want to get this all done today."

Kenny trotted back and forth happily. He didn't have a hod, but Mr. Teague made him believe a small bucket was better. "Maybe I should have been a bricklayer," Mr. Teague said. "It's nice easy work, and with a good helper like this —"

Kenny beamed. "But it makes me hungry," he said. "When do we eat?"

"When we're done," Bob spoke up. Then he laughed and gave Kenny a shove. "And it better be soon. I'm starved, too."

Working in the open air certainly gave you a tremendous appetite. Or maybe it wasn't just working in the open air, but working *together*. All the club members had been working lately — spading gardens, planting, weeding old flower beds, clearing lawns. But that had been each boy for himself. This was different. Here they were together, working on a group project. And having their fathers with them made it super.

Yes — this Saturday had turned out all right! . . . Even

if it did mean losing the day for jobs that would have paid money into the treasury.

For a while yesterday they had thought it was going to rain, and it had made them gloomy. Because they *had* to set up the piers this Saturday if the caboose was to be delivered in two weeks. Then, this morning, it had cleared, and now the sun was bright and high in the heavens; there was a slight nip in the air that made bending and stooping good exercise. And it was almost time to light the fire in the outdoor grill.

That was Bob's job. Kenny came over to watch him. "Remember, Kenny," Bob asked, "how just about this time last year we moved in and celebrated by having a supper out of doors, and you and your father came?"

Kenny nodded. "And I wouldn't eat the potato salad. But I would now!"

The Browns had only been in this house a year. It was a year that had flown, and yet, in another way, it seemed as if their moving from the little crowded green house had been long, long ago. It certainly had been the luckiest thing they ever did! Now they had a garden and a fireplace, and a big barn — that even had old lumber and a sleigh in it — and soon they would have a caboose! Sometimes Bob felt like pinching himself.

Suzie came running out of the barn, her daffodil-colored hair flying. Doctor Quack was having a hard time keeping up with her. "He did it, he did it!" she shouted at Bob.

"Did what?" Bob asked, his mind on the fire.

"Sat on his chair! I had two cookies and I gave them to him in little pieces, and he quacked every time. Just like a dog. . . . I mean, he quacked instead of barked."

"Gee, Suzie, that's great."

"Now I have Doctor Quack doing tricks, and Catten, and Rex."

"You ought to be an animal trainer," he teased her.

She said seriously, "Maybe I will be. I used to think I'd be a trapeze walker, or maybe a kindergarten teacher . . . But now I think I'll train animals to make money . . . and for fun."

"I wish I knew what *we* could do to make money," Orphie said, coming up just in time to hear the last part.

"We're doing all right," Bob said comfortingly. "Except we haven't anything in the treasury . . . what with buying the cinder blocks and paying for the trucking and the ca boose."

"Well, how much worse could it be?" Orphie demanded, but not at all gloomily. "I guess we'll think of something — besides weeding and fixing lawns and stuff . . . only I wish I knew what it was. We ought to have something we could do right now — or almost right now — so we'd have money on hand." He scratched his head thoughtfully. "You know, like a fair, or a show, or —"

"A show!" Suzie cried, her eyes bright. "An animal show!"

Bob and Orphie looked at each other and then at Suzie.

"Suzie, I think you've got something there!" Bob said excitedly. "You get an extra frankfurter."

"When?"

"When I cook it. . . . Listen, Orphie, we could have Suzie's animals, and Jan's Poke, and Matt's Towser —"

"That wouldn't be enough. I mean, if we had a really bang-up show that we charged admission for . . . But maybe *we* could be animals, too."

Bob pounded Orphie on the back. "Boy! What animals we could be!"

"Bob, come and help carry out the food, please!" his mother called from the house.

"I'll help," Orphie offered. "We'll tell the others while we eat."

"You don't know Mom's cooking," Bob said heartily. "You can't talk about *anything* while you eat her cooking!"

They set up card tables and brought out a few folding chairs. For the rest, they sat on piles of cinder blocks or on blankets on the ground. Bob grilled hamburgers and toasted franks. Mrs. Larssen had brought a pot of baked beans. Kenny's mother had made macaroni, and Matt's mother had made a bowl of coleslaw. Mrs. Brown had made a big pan of biscuits, two apple pies and a chocolate cake.

Kenny piled a plate high and retired to one end of the teeter-totter, so as not to be interrupted in the serious business of eating. Bob gathered the rest of the club around him

while he manned the grill, and told them of Suzie's idea —
and Orphie's addition.

"I'll be the front half of an elephump," Pete offered.

"What's an elephump?"

"Something like an elephant, goon, but different . . . as
different as we can make it."

"I'll be a diplodocus," Clint said smugly.

"A diplod — a whoosis?" Jan demanded.

"A diplodocus," Clint said. "Prehistoric. . . . That
means before your day, shrimp."

"We can't just *be* things, we have to *do* things," Orphie
said anxiously.

"Such as selling tickets?"

"That, too. . . . Pat, will you letter tickets for us?" Bob
called.

Pat, trying to manage a wedge of cake, said in a muffled
voice, "For what?"

"An animal show . . . to raise money for the caboose."

"Sure," she said; and added, after a moment, "for free
. . . this time."

The idea appealed to all of them. They'd have to work
up acts, of course, make sure their animals were letter per-
fect, and then invent something for themselves.

"When would we have it?"

"The sooner the better."

"Yes, but we'll have to rehearse . . . and do our other

jobs . . . and we'll have to get our mothers to make costumes . . . whatever we can't do ourselves —"

"Where would we have it?"

"In the barn, of course." Bob answered that one promptly.
"If it's good weather we could have it outdoors, but there's
always the barn in case."

Chip hadn't offered to be anything. "What are you going
to be, Chip?"

"I don't know," he said sullenly.

"Be yourself," Jan teased.

"I — I don't think Mom could sew a costume for me —"

"Why not?" Pete said easily. "The crazier the better."

"She won't be here. . . . She's going to Florida."

"How do you know she won't be here?" Clint said bel-
ligerently. "We haven't even set the date yet."

Chip looked miserable. But he stuck it out. "She's going
soon, and she's going to stay a month anyhow," he said.

Bob said hurriedly, "Well, we'll work out something.
. . . The main thing is we want to do it, and we'll have to
line up our acts, and sell tickets at school." He broke into
a wide grin. "Gosh, it ought to be good — and fun, too."

CHAPTER 8

The pike itself had to be neglected for a while. There just wasn't enough time for everything, and right now the main job was planning the interior of the clubhouse. Uncle Bill had brought them a scale drawing, and that made it easier.

The Browns' cellar rang with arguments and discussions on the club nights. Poring over the drawing, trying to imagine just how it would look in reality, they drew in the equipment for the workshop, the chairs, the space required for the pike . . . and then erased it; tried another grouping, erased that; tried a third time. . . .

They would have to redesign their pike, that was sure. The table they were using now was small, and since they would have so much more space available they wanted to put it to the best use. The amount of equipment on hand wasn't enough to take up all the space; but how should they apportion it so that it looked right, and made a good showing, and yet left them room to expand when they had the additional equipment? Then, too, they wanted to use the scenery they had — they would have to have so much more! — so as not to give a scrawny appearance to the whole pike outlay. They had to plan just what Bruce was to make, in order to fill in most realistically.

There were plenty of problems; but it was exciting. When the caboose actually came and was in place, they would be able to see how their plans had worked out — and, if necessary, change them. But you had to have a plan ready.

Buck Curtis and a helper brought the caboose on a platform trailer two weeks later. It was another Saturday, a rainy one, and chilly. Even so, when the truck rolled into the yard, half the neighborhood seemed to be gathered there in a matter of minutes.

Nobody could really believe that the big, bulky, dark red caboose was to be theirs. Not even when it was rolled gently off the truck, onto the stringers, and into place on the piers. It just didn't seem possible.

"Let's see inside, let's see inside!" the small fry demanded.

"Not till we have Open House!" Bob told them firmly, and no matter how they begged and pleaded, he kept to that. The club members had decided it was to be so. When they were all ready, they would have a show. Until then, nobody was to get inside.

Buck Curtis said, mopping his brow, "Any time the housing shortage gets serious, you can rent this."

"I'd rent it right now," his helper said, laughing. "Looks like it's got more room in it than the house I have!"

The driveway was rutted, there were deep muddy tracks where the platform truck had moved across the grass . . . but there the caboose stood, long and red and solid, with its four side windows, its little end platforms, its cupola raised above the central section . . . theirs! All theirs!

The club members swarmed inside, shutting the others out. Their excited talk and laughter made the echoes ring. Rain drummed on the roof, ran down the dirty windowpanes. They darted around, shouting and pointing. It really *was* like the drawing . . . only better, a thousand times better. The drawing was impersonal; this was real; they could smell the wood, touch the bunks, climb into the cupola. And how big it was! Bigger than they had imagined; bigger, even, than they had hoped. Big enough for everything!

"We'll have to tear out the upper bunks there —"

"Yeah, but carefully. That lumber will come in handy."

"And here where the letter rack is we can have the compartments Mr. Kendall made for us —"

"No, let's leave that, and put our compartments next the workbench —"

"We'll have our clubroom at this end, just the way we planned —"

"And leave the center section free, and put our pike at the other end."

"See, it's going to work out! If we have the control panel at that end, by the door, then the jump seat for the one who is working the control panel can be attached to the door! Neat!"

They swarmed toward the rear.

"The pike will be here — at the engineer's left, and across in front of him. And then, when we get money enough for new stuff" — Orphie sighed — "we'll have all this space down the other side to add to it. Oh boy!"

Clint snorted. "Why go at it in a small-time way? *I* say we should build the whole pike now, the way it's going to be."

"But we can't afford that now."

"You'd better do it my way. I know what I'm talking about — I'm older than the rest of you."

That was Clint — always trying to be the boss. He'd been doing it more and more often lately and they had a hard time talking him down.

Now they said, "Our way, we can take our time adding on. . . . And meanwhile, anyone who comes to see our pike can see the whole thing right here!"

"We might as well tear out the sink, too," Karl was saying practically, as he roamed around. "We can't use it, since we won't have water —"

"Come to think of it . . ." Bob said suddenly, and stopped. It was an awful thought. "We not only won't have water, but we won't have electricity, either. Unless we get hitched up, we can't run the pike."

"We would have to have an electrician do that," Skinny said slowly.

"More money!"

"Well, we've got to have it."

"Yes, but not right away," Orphie said hopefully. "We have plenty to do before we have a chance to run the pike, and meantime —"

"Meantime maybe we can think up a way to make more money."

Skinny told Mr. Yerkes the caboose was in place, and Mr. Yerkes came to see it. They made an exception for him and showed him around with pride. After all, Mr. Yerkes was sort of special, and he had been a lot of help. When he heard their latest problem, he didn't seem to think it was much of a problem after all.

"I have a friend who's an electrician," he said easily. "Maybe he will do it for you."

"Yes, but electricians charge a lot," Orphie said matter-of-factly. "We asked around. They're almost all the same. And it's a lot."

"This friend of mine, though," Mr. Yerkes said, smiling, "I rather think would make a special price."

"Why would he?"

"Because he's a model railroad fan, too! He'd be glad to help out brothers in distress."

They didn't bank on it too much, but it turned out to be true. Mr. Reifschneider was a short, stout man with stubby, capable hands and a nice grin. They watched him work and he explained what he was doing and why. It looked so easy! Bob said so.

"Sure, everything looks that way when you know how." He closed his kit. "And it *is*, when you know how. I bet you've found that out yourselves."

He tested the overhanging lamp he had arranged for them, and light sprang up. "Yep, it works. Thought it would! How much does it cost you fellas to run this outfit?"

They looked at one another blankly. "Why — uh, we don't know," Bob said.

"You don't know! That's good. Better find out. . . . *Somebody must be paying the bill, and I suspect it's your parents.*"

Somehow that had never occurred to them. Mr. Brown had let them use the current for their pike, and they had burned lights in the cellar workroom for hours on end. That was part of their expenses . . . but they hadn't figured on it. With an enlarged pike, with this new lighting, they would have added expense, and they ought to take care of it themselves. . . . It was one thing after another!

"How would we go about finding out?" Bob asked now. "How much it costs, I mean?"

"Two ways," Mr. Reifschneider said briskly. "You could have a separate meter installed — by the power company, of course — and meter your own. But that hardly seems worth while for this amount of current. Why don't you just get out your father's light bills for some months back, before you started, average 'em up, and then see what the difference is for those months you've been running the pike. That would give you a pretty close idea. Not accurate, of course, but close enough, I'd say."

When they had done that, they discovered that they had used approximately one dollar's worth of extra current for each of the two months. Mr. Brown, when they told him they'd like to pay up, said they should forget it — that was his contribution to the new club. But from now on, they insisted, they would pay their own way. Would he settle for a dollar monthly? That, they felt, ought to take care of all the electricity they might use.

Mr. Brown was agreeable. "Want a contract?" he said, laughing.

"Not if you don't," Bob answered, and they shook hands on it.

On the next Saturday — another half day gone for working on outside jobs! — the club members and their fathers put up the wooden siding to cover the piers and the empty space in between. They were all there this time — even Mr. Randolph. Mr. Randolph seemed a little ill at ease, but he was working right along with them, doing whatever was suggested.

Orphie nodded over his shoulder. "How come he's here?" he asked Bob, in a low voice so Chip wouldn't hear.

Bob said, in a low voice, too, "Oh, some of the men bowl at the same place Mr. Randolph does, and golf on the same course . . . and they've sort of been giving him the cold shoulder, Dad says. They told him what they thought of him, always ditching the jobs, so he took the hint and volunteered to come and help this time."

Chip seemed particularly happy about the fact that his father was actually there. He swaggered around, doing very little himself, but talking a lot.

"Come on, get busy," Clint grumbled.

Chip said airily, "I'm no good at nailing boards, never was. I might spoil things." He sat down on an overturned keg and went on talking.

The siding grew apace. It looked funny — all kinds of wood, and weathered to different shades. A house was being dismantled and they had picked up some of the lumber at a bargain price. Mr. Reifschneider had told them about it, and they had got there early and put in a bid — paid cash on the line, too — and the contractor had let them take it right away.

"It'll look swell, though, when it's painted," Bruce said happily. "I can hardly wait! I'll be doing that while you guys work on the interior."

"You think you're lucky?" Pete asked, with a grin.

"I know I am," Bruce said. "Bob's Uncle Bill said he'd help me. . . . I mean, tell me just where the wheels would be, and the journals and the tool box. Then he's going to draw them on for me, and I'll paint them. It'll look like the real thing."

"A lot better than this, anyhow," Orphie said, cautiously, and they all laughed.

"Yeah. Where *is* Uncle Bill, by the way?" Bob stood up, mopping sweat from his brow. "He promised to come early and lend a hand. . . . Not that we need him, but he's nice to have around."

"There he comes now," Suzie said. Suzie had an unerring eye for Uncle Bill. "Just turning in the drive." She ran forward, dragging a reluctant Doctor Quack on a leash. "Uncle Bill, Uncle Bill, come see what I've got in the barn!"

He got out of his car and picked her up, giving her a giant hug. Doctor Quack quacked indignantly at being left out.

"Wait till you see what Aunt Meg and *I've* got — in the hospital!" he shouted.

"In the hospital?" Suzie squeaked excitedly. "What — what?"

The boys stopped working, and Bob came tearing up.

"You mean —"

"A new cousin for you!" Uncle Bill cried. "Handsomest boy you ever saw in the world. Two weeks early, but he weighs seven pounds, three ounces. Young Bill, Junior."

"Gosh!" Bob said, his eyes shining. "That's great, Uncle Bill. Say, won't *he* enjoy the pike and the caboose . . . when he's older, I mean?"

CHAPTER 9

Mother put it up to them.

"When Aunt Meg's ready to come home from the hospital," she said, "do you think you could do without me for a week?"

"A *week?* What for?" It was a pretty bleak prospect.

"Well, she's a new mother and there are lots of things she will want to know. And I can keep house for her so that she has time to rest and get acquainted with her baby." Mother beamed at them each in turn. "I *know* you can do it. And it would make me so happy!"

Of course, after that, there wasn't much they could do but say Yes. Mother had planned it all out, it seemed. "Suzie can stay at Mrs. Grainger's —"

"Poor Kenny!" Bob grinned. "It serves him right, though. We had him staying here with *us* last year."

"I like Kenny," Suzie spoke up. "He does what I want . . . mostly."

"And you're a nice little cook, Pat," Mother went on. "I'll leave menus and recipes if you want me to . . . or you can work them out yourself. Bob can cook outdoor style once in a while, if he likes . . . and between you you can do the washing up and such cleaning as needs to be done. I'll get Mrs. Hogan in for the heavy work and the laundry. I imagine Wayne will look after his own room for that week. I'll ask him."

"Never mind, Mother," Pat spoke up. "I can do his room, too . . . after school if I don't get it done before."

"Oh, you don't need to overwork yourself," Bob said, giving her a brotherly poke. "I'll do it one day and you can do it the next." He had a sudden thought. "If Mom's gone seven days, though, *you* start. That gives you four days and me three."

"All right, then," Pat shot back good-naturedly. *"You* can start with the dishes."

Bob had another thought, but he kept it to himself. If he was going to help with the house, he wouldn't have time to do outside jobs that earned money. Well, it was one of those things. . . . All he could hope was that his mother wouldn't have to stay away longer than a week.

They got along pretty well. Everybody helped getting breakfast, which made it easy, and Pat and Bob packed their own school lunches. Father bought supplies and brought them home. The dusting was rather sketchy, but nobody minded. And the cooking was fun.

Of course, they had some accidents. One night Pat forgot to put baking powder in the biscuits, but Father said he rather liked flat biscuits — they were easier to eat, if your teeth held out. And Mr. Kendall told her it was sort of like hardtack, and if sailors could live on hardtack for months he guessed they could stand it for one night. Then Bob burned the hamburgers, and by the time he'd scraped off the black there wasn't much left. But they opened a can of beans and that helped. He put too much wax on the floors in certain places and had to take it up with the flat side of a knife, and Pat set the iron too high and scorched some rayon clothes.

But altogether they got on pretty well. It made funny things to tell — that is, *some* things did — when their mother telephoned and when they went to see the Jarvises. The first time they saw the new baby, though, they had a hard time keeping their faces straight. Uncle Bill and Aunt Meg were certainly funny . . . *that* squirmy, red-faced bundle with its eyes all screwed up, was supposed to be handsome? Why, Suzie hadn't looked like that.

Aunt Meg breathed, "Isn't he *wonderful?*" And Uncle Bill slapped Bob on the shoulder. "I think he looks like you — lucky fella." It was hard to take. But he *was* a new cousin, their first one.

Mother stayed ten days instead of a week, and it was the longest ten days of their lives. Mr. Kendall took to eating out the last three nights. He said he had business downtown, but they knew better.

They slicked the house and had everything shining when she returned. Father brought her a dozen pink roses and Mr.

Kendall had a huge box of candy. "I was never gladder to see anyone!" he said fervently. "And not just because of your cooking, either!"

"How's the animal show going?" Mother asked, when she had settled into the big chair and they were all sitting around at her feet. It certainly made a difference to have her home.

"Wait till you see it!" Bob chortled. "Suzie has her animals all trained, and the costumes are the zaniest ever. You're to have a special box seat!" Pat giggled, and he shot her a silencing glance.

It *was* just that: an upended box, on which they had put a cushion. The rest of the audience had to sit on planks laid on sawbucks.

"Maybe we ought to clean the barn — some," Pat had said doubtfully.

Bob had looked up into the dim, cobwebby rafters and vetoed it quickly. "It's a barn, and it ought to look like a barn. It's not everybody can offer a show in a barn. Forget it!"

She was glad to. She and Bonnie were to be permitted to sell tickets because the entire club was taking part in the show. Even Kenny had a part — the rear end of the brontosaurus. They had had to give up the diplodocus after looking it up in a book. Its front feet were small, so that two people couldn't get inside the costume.

It was a good thing they had decided to have the show in the barn after all, for on that day it was chilly and overcast. The uncertain weather didn't keep away the crowd, though.

Everybody came . . . schoolmates by the dozen, parents, friends of parents, neighbors, and people they had never seen who bought tickets at the door. Pat ran out of printed ones, and had to tear up pieces of colored paper and mark them 25 *cents — paid,* as fast as she could write.

The animal performers were hidden in the rear of the barn, and it was pretty noisy. The boys were dressing in the box stalls, and they were crowded. When all the seats were taken, and the small fry in the front row began stamping and shouting, Bob opened the show.

As ringmaster, he wore a cutaway coat and a tall silk hat that had belonged to Matt's grandfather. His whip was almost as tall as himself, with a long braided cord attached to it. He came out wearing his hat, the hatband stuffed with tissue paper so it wouldn't fall over his eyes.

"Ladeeez and gentlemen!" he shouted, in the best master-of-ceremonies style. "You are about to see the greatest show in town, the greatest show in the state; in fact, the greatest show in the nation! We have assembled for your delight one of the finest collections of trained and wild animals ever to be gathered under one roof. First of all: Miss Suzanne Brown, with the only trained duck in the world — Doctor Quack!"

He moved aside, took off his hat, placed it on a stool and sat down on it. The hat collapsed (it was a collapsible hat) and laughter swept over the barn. Suzie tripped out, wearing a pink dress and ballet slippers, her golden hair flying like a cloud. Doctor Quack waddled beside her. She placed a chair and told the audience sweetly, "Doctor Quack is the only duck in the world who can sit on a chair. Sit on the chair, Doctor Quack!"

The duck acted as if he had never heard the words before. His little eyes roved over the audience, he waddled back and forth, back and forth, and suddenly, stretching his neck, he made a rush for Pete, who was standing on the sidelines, and nipped him in the ankle. Pete let out a bellow of rage and surprise, and the audience howled. They thought it was part of the show.

Suzie said, "He wasn't supposed to do that. . . . Doctor Quack, you are acting very bad. Come here now, and sit on the chair." But Doctor Quack simply wouldn't. He had done it over and over again in the past week, but by this time he was apparently tired of the trick, and refused to do it.

"Oh well," Suzie told the assembled audience, with her sweetest smile, "I have lots of other animals who can do tricks, and it just shows how smart Doctor Quack really is. . . . He doesn't do things unless he wants to!"

Jan brought out his Poke, a large sad-eyed dog who, on command, rested his elbows on the ground, raising his rear ridiculously in the air, rolled his eyes and prayed. Matt's Towser, a beautiful white Spitz with pointed ears and plumy tail, his collar bedecked with a bright red ribbon, jumped through a hoop, turned around, and jumped through again. His tongue hung out, his eyes glittered. And when his trick

was over he ran around in circles of joy. He was a born actor.

Suzie came back then with Catten, who, at a word from her, sat up on her haunches. When she was given a piece of meat, she ate it daintily, holding it up between her paws. Suzie beamed, and hugged Catten to her. "That's only *one* of the things she can do," she said happily.

And Rex outdid himself, wiping his feet on a doormat. Everybody loved that. First he had some morsels to eat, then Suzie told him to go and wipe his feet, and then his whiskers. *Nobody* had seen a dog do that, and Rex was so delighted with their applause that he did both tricks over again.

Bob had worked out a spiel for everything. "And now —" he shouted, jumping up, punching his collapsible hat into shape again and cocking it on his head at a rakish angle — "and now for the wild animals we have brought you at great trouble and expense! Prepare yourselves, hold on to your seats! You've never seen anything like it! Open the cage," he ordered in a voice that echoed in the barn, "and let out the man-eating lion — a ferocious beast of the jungle, the fiercest lion in captivity!"

Little Karen Holt, sitting in the first row, piped up, "Am I supposed to be afraid?"

"No, no," Bob said grandly, "this lion does not care for little girls. He only eats *men!* Bring him on!" Out of the stall shambled a lion with big feet and a straw mane. His head swung from side to side and he roared loudly. Bob brandished his whip and, at the same time, used a pair of clackers in his other hand. It made the whip sound frightening as it sailed through the air, and the tip landed on the lion's lumpy body. At this the lion's roar broke off suddenly, and he howled plaintively. Bob chased him around the arena.

The lion's stary glass eyes seemed to fasten first on one person and then another when he roared. Then the whip would descend, and he would let out a long *Owwwww!* and gingerly rub the sore spot with one great paw, while the audience shrieked.

"He's looking for a man to eat!" Bob yelled. "And *here* is the man!" He held up a gingerbread man in one hand, and with that the lion made a lunge, grabbed the gingerbread cookie, and collapsed on the floor to growl over it.

It was a hilarious afternoon. "The only trained aerial-performing monkey!" Bob announced. "Straight from the heart of Africa!"

Pete Daly limped on in an ill-fitting gray flannel monkey suit with a silly monkey false face. With great-to-do, he attempted to jump onto the trapeze bar. Time and again he tried, and failed, each time acting sillier than the last. Finally he got a wooden crate from the side lines, climbed on that, and swung his long arms over the bar, resting his chin on it as if to ask what he should do next. But once he was up, he did all kinds of tricks that convulsed the guests.

"The kangy-roo!" Bob cried dramatically. "The only kangy-roo in captivity that sells kangy-bars! Step right up and see for yourselves!" And sure enough, out of its silly pouch, made of a sewing bag set inside the suit, the kangy-roo dispensed chocolate bars and peanuts and chewing gum, and even made change. When the pouch was empty, it did a side-splitting pantomime of searching for more.

"And now," Bob shouted, "the climax of the afternoon! A real, live brontosaurus! Never before seen in these or any other parts! Found frozen in a distant glacier, it was thawed out with atomic power, and trained over a long period of years. Never before has a brontosaurus been seen in these regions, and after this afternoon it will return to its frozen state in the glacier; so watch carefully!"

Clint was the tall front half, and Kenny the short rear. The long stuffed tail spread out along the floor, supposedly managed by Kenny. He had done all right in rehearsal, but now, excited by his importance, he took three steps to Clint's two, and the effect was so funny it had the audience in stitches.

"Hey, wait a minute, something's caught!" came in unmistakable Kenny tones from the back half of the brontosaurus. Clint let out a loud, "*Shhh*, you dope!" and Kenny took three more running steps. The long tail, snagged on a nail, was yanked off, and the rear of Kenny's blue jeans was plainly seen. It brought down the house. Even Bob forgot his part and wiped his streaming eyes, while he bent double laughing. That Kenny! You could always count on him to foul things up, but this time it was really funny.

The afternoon was a big success. "I haven't laughed so

hard in a month of Sundays," some of the parents said. And the kids went around joking and poking the "animals" and giving the real ones bits of crackers and candy and a lot of praise. Everybody seemed to think he had had his quarter's worth, especially when it was discovered that cookies and punch were free. That is, one cookie and one cup of punch to each ticket holder.

"Free!" Sam Dawson sang out. "What's wrong with it?"

Nothing was the matter with it, as he found out. The girls manned the punch bowl (which was just a gallon bucket, draped with pretty paper), and handed out the paper cups full of pink punch. The cookies disappeared like magic. Crumbs were all over the barn, but there was nothing that a good sweeping wouldn't take care of.

The actors gathered after the last guests had gone. "Nobody wanted to go home," Orphie said happily. "That shows it was good."

"And how much did we make?" Jan demanded, wiping his perspiring face.

Orphie and Pat counted up. "Taking out the cost of the refreshments, and the cups and — and — well, that's all — we made twenty dollars and fifty cents."

"Whee! Not bad!"

"Not bad? It's swell! Think of what twenty dollars will buy!"

They looked over at the caboose. . . . Twenty dollars wouldn't go too far, but they were on their way.

CHAPTER 10

It was hot work, picking berries. The sweat ran off Bob's face. It was running down the back of his neck, too; his shirt was wet. He looked at the row of baskets at his feet, and the smell of ripe strawberries was too much for him. He popped one of them into his mouth.

Mr. Robbins had sent a hurry call for helpers. The berries were ready and there weren't enough men available. Bob had jumped at the chance, and asked Buck Curtis to drop him off on his way into town. Skinny and Karl and Clint and Bruce had bicycles, and they said they'd come, too. As a team they were doing very well. And it was nice pay. Chip had a bike, but he hadn't come.

It was a good thing the end of the school year was in sight. They were so busy they met themselves going and coming! Only two more weeks to go and they'd be graduating. All except Clint, who was older; he was in the first year of High. When school was out, though, they'd be able to go ahead with their money-earning plans, and — best of all — devote more time to cleaning and rearranging the caboose interior and building their new pike.

Bob called down the row, "Mrs. Hogan wants us for currants later. Did you see Mrs. Villiers about her lawn, Bruce?"

"Yep."

"I got a job cleaning the Merkel cellar," Karl offered. He grinned. "It's nice and *cool* down there!"

They had mowed lawns; they had weeded vegetable gardens; they had washed windows and polished cars. Several of them had occasional jobs as errand boys, because of their bikes. They could always get jobs with other farmers in the neighborhood to help harvest berry crops. The Caboose Club fund was growing nicely. It would have grown faster if they had put all the money they earned into it. But most of them *had* always earned their own spending money — all except Chip, of course — and it wasn't fair to expect them to turn over everything to the fund. It was hard to wait, though . . . there was so much they wanted to do, and everything cost so much.

Karl wiped an arm across his forehead. "Boy, I feel as red as a strawberry myself!"

"Cheer up, this is going to be a ten-dollar job. Don't forget the meeting tonight."

"I hope your Mom makes a tall pitcher of lemonade. . . . I'm dry to my toes."

There was a lot to talk about, and to do. They had already

taken out the upper berths at the pike end of the caboose.
. . . They had done it very carefully, because they needed
whatever lumber they could salvage.

One of the bunks at the sink end had been covered over to
make a workbench. They had left the letter rack, and had
hung a red-handled hatchet in the bracket where the fire ax
had been. They had installed a drain for the sink — which
they had decided to keep, after all — but the water still had
to be toted in buckets. Kenny was good for that job. If he was
going to hang around, he might as well be put to some use,
and there wasn't much harm he could do toting water, except
spill it.

They had made the foundation for their new pike, too —
using their old table top, enlarging it and bracing it with
scrap lumber. Small strips of the scrap were used for track-
board. That left open spaces, of course . . . but these were
to be covered by scenery, anyhow. Tonight was the night
Bruce had promised to bring all the scenery he had been
making at home, and they would set it in place, according to
the plan.

The old pike had been dismantled and most of the materials used for the new. But as the new pike began to take
shape, the boys were appalled to discover that their trains
looked awfully small and lost on the expanse that was now
available. They still had only two engines, so they could
have only two trains. They were going to have to do a lot of
filling in.

They had decided that they could put in a small spur of track to fill some of that large open space. Leaving some freight cars on the spur would help. The trouble was, they didn't have the freight cars! There wasn't time to make them, and Chip offered to buy a few of the cheaper plastic ones. He had done a good job, too, of changing them with small additions and painting them to look like the real thing.

They were all tired that evening after the berry picking, but some bottles of Coke helped, and they set to work laying track and getting the wiring completed, working in teams so as to hurry matters along.

"We've got to get finished so we can have our railroad show," Orphie said anxiously. "A couple of more weeks and school will be out. We ought to set a date so we can get a notice on the bulletin board."

The railroad show was a kind of goal. With all their track laid, the caboose slicked up, the cars in order, they would throw open the caboose for the first time and have a real Open House.

"Do you charge admission, though, for an Open House?" Karl demanded.

"We do," Jan returned swiftly.

"Nobody needs to come if he isn't willing to pay thirty-five cents," Matt said gruffly. "After all, we're not *makin'* 'em. And there are plenty of kids — and grownups, too — who are dying to see inside this clubhouse."

"Do you think we ought to charge as much as thirty-five cents, though, for the little kids?"

"Sure. They make more trouble, they'll be into everything."

"We'll station 'guards' all along the caboose, so they'll have to keep their hands off."

"Who's going to run the control panel that day?" Clint asked.

"Whosever turn it is."

"I ought to run it," Clint said. "I'm the oldest."

"We go by turns," Bob said sternly. "You know that. We always have. . . . If we can get the wiring finished, we'll run it tonight. Dad and Mr. Kendall want to see the run. . . . Hey, Bruce, need some help there?"

Bruce shook his head. He was clamping his tongue between his teeth, trying to get the "cliffs" of the miniature quarry firmly anchored. It was pretty wonderful what he had done — almost all on his own.

"*We*'ve been doing all the hard work," Clint grumbled, "while he has a good time." He looked around to where Chip was blissfully working over a small building. "Him and Chip. . . ."

Chip raised his head. "Anybody can do what *you're* doing," he said with his usual arrogance, "but Bruce and I are different. Anyhow, I *like* doing what I'm doing, and that's all I'm going to do — except run the panel when it's ready."

Bob sighed. Chip certainly made fine buildings, and some of the houses in the village along the pike were actual replicas of their own homes. But he wasn't a good team member. He never would drop what he liked doing in order to do what *needed* doing. Lots of the fellows had grumbled about it, but that didn't make any difference to Chip. He certainly didn't have the proper club spirit.

When it was time to call in Mr. Brown and Mr. Kendall, they found that Uncle Bill had come over. "Here's a present," he said tossing a package on the table. Bob undid it and let out a whoop of joy. "An engineer's cap!" he shouted. "It looks like a real one!"

"Right off the head of Andrew McCarry," Uncle Bill said happily. "With the compliments of the Jersey Central to the Big Ten Railroad. Whose turn is it to wear it?"

"Pete's," Bob said, trying to keep a little envy out of his voice. It would have been fun to be the first one.

Pete put the cap on proudly. It fell over his ears somewhat so he stuffed the inside with paper. The tall crown seemed very large and the long visor shaded his intent face as he bent over the control panel.

"Hey," Chip called out, "why don't you let me run that tonight?"

"It's not your turn."

"Who cares about turns? *I* ought to run the pike — I've put more money into it than all the rest of you together."

"*Money* — not work," Pete shot out unexpectedly. It was

what they were all thinking, but the words had a queer sound. Somehow, they wished they had not been said.

"You'll have to take your turn like the rest of us," Bob told him. "And it's Pete's tonight."

"You guys make me sick!" Chip flung out. He whirled around, nearly brushing a couple of cars off the table.

"Act your age!" Jan said in a sarcastic voice.

Pete called, "Ready?" He turned on the current. . . . The trains began to move.

It helped to ease the strain. You couldn't stay mad, or be too upset, watching the work of months take form. Everything went fine. . . . Mr. Brown and Mr. Kendall were loud in their praises. They'd have a show worth seeing. Looking down at the pike, Bob felt his face flushing with pleasure. This had all started with Mr. Teague's gift of a caboose kit. And look how far they had come!

That one notice on the school bulletin board pulled a large return. It seemed to the Big Tenners that half the school turned out. And, of course, curiosity about the inside of the caboose was at fever pitch. There had been a good writeup in the local paper.

Had *that* been a surprise — when a reporter called up and asked if he could have a sneak preview! He wouldn't give away the details, he said, and he had heard about their project from Mr. Yerkes. They had the clipping pasted on the wall above the sink where they could read it every time they went to wash their hands or get a drink. And all the visitors could see it, too, along with their pictures.

Mr. Yerkes was among the first to come. "You go in for free," they told him. "You're a real friend of the club; you helped us a lot."

"Not at all," he said heartily. "I had as much fun as you had. Maybe more. I want to pay like everybody else."

The boys were stationed every few feet. They kept an eagle-eyed watch so that nothing was touched or damaged. Orphie, wearing the engineer's cap, was at the control panel, and he certainly put on a good show. The boys took turns explaining how the outfit was run, and how it was made. The grownups wandered around the caboose and wished they had had a place like this when *they* were kids . . . and the kids were openmouthed and almost speechless with envy.

"Lemme join; lemme, please!" the members heard on all sides. It was hard telling them that the membership was full.

Everything went beautifully. The trains ran without a hitch; the timetable Chip had drawn up had been gone over and over for flaws, and they had had practice runs for a week.

"Look at the way it goes over the bridge!"

"And watch 'em couple and uncouple!"

"Isn't that a super station?"

"Yeah, but the coalyard . . . it even looks like real coal."

"And the lumberyard, and the lumber — it's all so tiny —"

"And the rocks, and the little lake, and the silos —"

Bob left the hubbub and went over to Karl. "Where's Chip? He didn't turn up this afternoon, either."

Karl shrugged. "Who knows? We could use him. We're all as busy as one-armed paper hangers."

People asked if those were the markings of real railroads on their cars; they wanted to know how Bruce had made that cluster of trees; they asked about the water tower (which was made out of a tin can), and the little bridges. They wanted to see the switch engine perform again and again.

The boys explained that the railroad was far from complete. When they had more money and more time, they would extend the pike all the way across the end of the caboose. They would have granaries and a complete village, they would have a tunnel, and maybe a mine.

"You'll put my outfit in the shade," Mr. Yerkes said with a chuckle. "After all, you have a lot more years ahead of you than I have."

When it was over, they had netted more than forty dollars. It was hard to believe. Orphie counted the money a second time to make sure. When the last visitors had left, the last child had been thrust out firmly, they closed the doors and called a club meeting.

Almost at once Clint said, "Now that we're a real club, with a clubhouse and everything, I think we ought to have officers."

It sounded all right to the others. "Sure," they said, happy but tired.

131

"We ought to have a president. Somebody who is a real leader," Clint insisted.

"Like you?" Pete laughed.

Clint flushed. "Why not?"

The boys pretended not to hear him. "Well, let's get going," Skinny remarked.

Matt was made chairman for the time being. Pete popped up at once and nominated Bob for president. Karl moved that the nominations be closed and that the secretary cast the ballot.

The boys laughed. "We haven't got any secretary!"

"Okay, then, we'll put it to a vote. . . . All in favor, say Aye!"

There was a thunder of Ayes. Bob felt his face grow red, and his chest hurt. They really wanted him for president!

There was no doubt about who would be treasurer. Orphie had done a swell job of taking care of the money.

"And let's not *have* a secretary!" Jan shouted. "Who wants to listen to minutes? We don't need them — we *know* what happened."

"But we ought to have a constitution, so everything is on a regular basis, and we have something to refer to."

"Okay, we voted you in," Pete said. "You name a committee."

Bob took the chair. "Thanks," he said gruffly. "I don't think we have to get stuffy about this officer business. But I'll do my best for the club. Pete, how about you being on the constitution committee? And Jan and Matt. Draw one up and maybe we can vote on it at the next meeting."

A voice came from the doorway. "Is the mob gone?"

They wheeled, and saw Chip standing there.

"Well! Where were *you*?" they demanded. "Why weren't you here to help handle the crowd?"

"I don't like crowds," Chip said with a scornful air. He tossed his cap onto the floor, as usual. "I went to the movies."

"All right, if you don't like crowds, what were you doing in the movies?" Bruce said quietly.

Clint stood up. "Yeah, you gold-bricker, you, I had to do double duty because you weren't here." He turned to the others. "What's more," he said, his voice getting louder and louder, "he hasn't done his share all the way through with this caboose. And *he* was the one who said we should get it. I haven't seen *him* working himself to the bone for it! He gets the fun and we get the work. Him and his money!"

They stared at Clint. He was shouting. Of course, it was the way most of them had felt about Chip at one time or another — but the way Clint said it gave it an ugly sound.

"All right!" Chip was shouting, too. "Me and my money! Try and get along without us! I notice you're always glad to have the money, anyway!"

Maybe he had a guilty feeling. Maybe Clint was getting under his skin. But this was no way for club members to act! "That's enough of that kind of talk," Bob said firmly. "Quit it, now, and let's get at the business."

"Yeah, pipe down, both of you," the others ordered.

"You won't shut me up like that!" Chip exploded. "You're a bunch of saps, that's what, to work so hard all the time. And for what? Nothing but a dumb club!" While they stared at him, he flung open the door and rushed out.

Had he taken leave of his senses? The high good spirits they had been in after the show were flattened to the floor. They sat in absolute silence for a minute, and then Clint said:

"He's nothing but a sorehead. He's made a lot of trouble in here. Are we going to keep on taking it? Why don't we boot him out?"

They sat there, stunned. To feel that Chip ought to go was one thing, to have it said out loud was another. But they would have to make the decision. It was a hard one to make. Chip's money *had* been welcome. Wasn't that the main reason why they had asked him in the first place? Moreover, he owned so much of the equipment. They looked around. All those cars . . . The tools he had bought, the files and pliers . . . All the little houses and buildings he had made . . . If he took those away, there wouldn't be much left of their pike. Somebody said as much, when they finally decided to expel him from the Club.

"But we can build it up again," Karl said stoutly. "How are we going to let him know he's out — write to him?"

It was terribly difficult. They bit their pencils, they crossed out words, crossed out lines, wrote them in again.

"We can't say that — we don't want to sound mad — we want to be sort of, well — dignified. . . ."

They worked hard over it. Now they wished they had a secretary. "You make a good copy of it, Jan; you write a good hand."

Jan, muttering, made a copy. "How are we going to get it to him? Mail it?"

"No," said Matt, "Pete and I go right by his house. We'll leave it under his door."

Pete quipped hollowly, "Save a three-cent stamp that way." But nobody felt like laughing.

When it was done, Bob turned out the lights and they filed out of the caboose. The boys said subdued good-nights — they felt queer.

Mr. Brown looked up when Bob came into the living room.

"What's the matter? Are you feeling pooped from the big day?"

Bob managed a sickly grin. "I guess so," he said and quickly, before his father could ask any more, went upstairs and got into bed as fast as he could.

He fell asleep at once, but it wasn't a good sleep. He tossed and turned and had one jumbled dream after another. In one of them he heard his father calling, calling. He woke up and listened. Maybe he *had* called. It was still dark. Maybe the house was on fire!

He leaped out of bed and rushed to the door.

His father and Mr. Kendall were running down the stairs. Bob, his heart in his mouth, rushed after them.

"What's the matter?" he called anxiously.

"We heard something," his father answered. He opened the back door and raced out of the house. There was just light enough to see a slim figure slip through the hedge toward Kenny's house, and then disappear.

There woud be no chance to catch him. "Where did he come from?" Bob asked.

"From the caboose. Come along."

Mr. Kendall had a flashlight. They moved swiftly across the yard and went up the steps of the caboose. The door was unlocked. Now that's queer, Bob thought. I know I locked it. I was the last to leave. I know it. . . . Then Mr. Brown opened the door and they all stepped through. Mr. Kendall beamed his flashlight over the interior.

Bob let out a groan. The clubroom end was a shambles. The worktable was heavily gashed. Tools were scattered over the floor. Two of the chairs were upended; one of them had a broken leg.

They switched on the overhanging light. In the glare it was worse. Bob ran to the other end and cast a frenzied look over the pike. Thank goodness, not much damage there that he could see! A couple of overturned cars . . . It seemed almost as if the intruder had been interrupted before he went too far. He had made too much noise and Bob's father had heard him.

Mr. Kendall pointed to the wall bracket where the hatchet was supposed to hang. It wasn't there. "That must be what he used," he said. But the hatchet was nowhere to be seen.

Bob straightened up slowly. There was a lump in his throat that he couldn't swallow. Their caboose! Their wonderful caboose!

Then he saw his father stoop to pick up something from the floor. It was Chip's cap.

CHAPTER 11

Next morning Bob called Orphie. "Come over, quick. Something's happened."

"But it's Sunday!" Orphie cried.

"I know. I'm calling all the others — all except Chip. We've got to have an emergency meeting. Hurry up, will you?"

They all came, worried by Bob's tone and by the fact that he wouldn't say what it was. When he opened the caboose door and they saw the damage, their anger flared.

"It was Chip all right — if his cap was there!"

"He could get in easy. We all have keys, and he hadn't turned his in."

"The way he walked out last night, you'd almost know he had something mean in mind."

"But *why?* Why did he want to do that to our caboose and the pike?"

"Don't you see? He found our note, and it made him hopping mad, and he wanted to have revenge on us. Golly! He's a stinker!"

"Have the police been here?"

"Yes," Bob answered, "right away. But they said there wasn't much to go on. There was no use fingerprinting — with all those people here yesterday handling things, and Dad and Mr. Kendall and I had all touched the doorknob. When they found our hatchet in the empty lot back of Kenny's, the handle had been wiped, they said."

"That proves it. He didn't want to be caught."

"What are we going to do?"

"Can we come in and see?" Pat asked. Bonnie had come over with Bruce and the two of them stood in the doorway.

"Later," Bob said, "when we've left. We've got to have a meeting now."

"There are all kinds of people going by and asking what happened," Pat said with relish. "They know about it somehow. I guess some of them heard the police car arrive last night."

"Well, keep 'em out," Bob ordered. "We're busy."

He brought the meeting to order but it was hard to keep it there. Mr. Randolph, several of them decided angrily, must be made to pay for the damage. Most of them agreed. But something bothered Bob.

"We don't really *know* that Chip did it," he said slowly.

"Oh, don't we?" Clint argued heatedly. "What's the matter with you? That's his cap, isn't it? And he stalked out on us, and we wrote him that note. . . . What more do you want, anyhow?"

"Yeah," the others shouted. "It's as clear as anything. Who else would have done it but Chip?"

"How much can we charge him for?" Bruce asked worriedly. "Just materials alone — or materials and time? . . . Even then, it probably won't cover the damage."

"What it costs to repair and replace," Karl said sternly. "That's only fair."

They made a hurried estimate, but it was difficult. Orphie wrote it down and made out a formal bill.

"We'll take it over right now," Jan said. "We'll all go together, so we can tell him what we think of him."

It was a solemn file of boys that walked down the street and across the field to Chip's house. Chip himself answered the bell, and somehow they hadn't expected that. He seemed utterly astonished to see them . . . or else he was putting on a good act.

They could see Mr. Randolph in the dining room and they stalked past Chip. Bob was in the lead. They strode into the dining room to where Mr. Randolph sat alone at the breakfast table, and Pete closed the door firmly. "You stay out of this," he said sternly to the amazed Chip, who was so surprised he made no effort to get in.

"What is all this?" Mr. Randolph asked in an annoyed fashion. He wiped his mouth on a napkin, threw it down, and turned to face the boys.

Bob explained soberly what had happened and why they

were there. Mr. Randolph's face got redder and redder. He looked as if he would explode.

"You kids have a nerve coming here and serving me with this bill!" he said furiously. "This is a fine way to try to get money out of me! But I won't go a step further till Chip's called in."

He had not said he didn't think Chip had done it. He just wanted to have Chip's word that he was innocent, so he would have more on his side. The boys sensed that.

"All right, we'll call him in," Bob said. He opened the door and Chip almost fell into the room.

"You're a fine bunch of pals!" he shouted. "You know I never did a thing like that!"

But he could have. And all the evidence pointed to him. Why shouldn't they think so? They reminded him how mad he had been, how he wouldn't cooperate lots of times on club projects, how he was always doing what he wanted to do . . .

"And you've been caught now a couple of times shooting out street lights, and had to go before the judge," Clint said with emphasis, pointing at him.

"Then, last night," Karl added, "when we put you out of the club, you got so mad you wanted to get even with us, so you tried to wreck the clubhouse —"

"I did not!" Chip's voice was shrill with panic, his eyes darted from one to the other. He certainly sounded guilty. "I wasn't anywhere near the caboose!"

"You mean to say you didn't come back?" Bob demanded. "Why, I saw you, Chip. I saw you, running away."

He hadn't meant to put it quite like that. What he had wanted to say was that he had seen a dim shape running through Kenny's yard and into the blackness, and it could have been Chip. With all the evidence they had at the caboose, it must have been Chip.

Chip suddenly went to pieces. He said miserably, "I — I did go back. . . ."

"Yah! You see?" It was a kind of chorus.

Mr. Randolph shouted, "Now, look here —"

"You went back and hacked up the place," Matt stated.

"No, I didn't, I tell you! I didn't! But after I got the note and read it — I saw Pete and Matt deliver it — I was so mad I could have — I could have . . . Then, after a while" — his voice sank and he dropped his head, twisting his hands together, his fingers weaving and breaking and weaving — "I sort of — well, I felt sorry. I got to thinking what good times we'd had together, working on the pike —"

"*You* only worked on the buildings most of the time —"

"I know. . . . But that was what I did best, and I wasn't as good as the rest of you guys at the pike and the cars and things —"

"Well," Skinny said implacably. "So then what?"

"Well, then," Chip said dully, "I decided to go over and have one more look. In the note you said I had to return the key, so I still had it. I was going to return it later. . . . And

I went over. I — I was keen about the caboose, and the pike, and everything. I just wanted to see it again. 'l'hat was all. So I went in and looked around, and wished . . . That's all I did. Then I went out and came home. Honest."

Nobody believed him. Bob didn't, and one look at the faces of the others told him that they didn't, either. Even Mr. Randolph didn't. His turkey-red face was still turkey-red, and he kept glaring at Chip, as if he were angriest of all at his son for getting himself and his father into this pickle.

He banged his fist on the table and stood up. "I've had enough of this nonsense — coming here, disturbing my Sunday morning with a cock-and-bull story like that. Somebody chopped up part of your workroom and the pike. Okay, I'll pay the bill — regardless of who did it — *on condition* —"

Bob said coldly, "On condition, what?"

"On condition that you take Chip back into the club and forget this whole business. Get the place fixed up and let's have an end to this."

Bob's heart sank. He didn't know what he had expected, but not this. Why did Mr. Randolph think that he could buy everything? That's where Chip got that attitude. But he couldn't buy Chip's return to the club. That was asking too much.

"No," he said, "we can't do that."

"We don't *want* him back," the others said loudly.

Chip looked around the circle of angry faces. He flung back his head and his eyes flashed. "All right," he said and

143

his voice was louder than all of theirs together, "all right, and I don't want to go back. I wouldn't go back on a bet! Keep your old club — I don't want to belong to it!"

They were all so intent on Chip that they didn't hear footsteps in the hall, and before they knew it there was Bonnie. She had been running, and she was breathless.

"Wait!" she cried. "Listen!" Her breath came in gasps. "Pat and I went into the caboose after you left, and we were looking around and I noticed something — so when the police came back just now to have another look, I showed them what I had found, and asked if that couldn't be so, and they said it could, so I ran all the way over here to tell you."

"Well, for Pete's sake, *what is it?*"

"It means Chip didn't do it!" she said triumphantly.

"But what? What did you see?" Girls were the limit.

"Just that" — she drew a deep breath — "that whoever used the hatchet was left-handed. . . . The way the cuts were slanted in the wood of the worktable top showed it was done by a left-handed person. And everybody knows Chip is *right*-handed!"

A swift, awful silence fell. What Bonnie had said was sinking in. Everybody did know that Chip was right-handed. That was true. They all were. All except Clint. . . . They turned to stare at Clint. He was the only southpaw in the group.

"Yes, *he's* left-handed," Bonnie said, speaking what was

in their minds for them. "I remember I noticed it whenever I watched him working on things."

Clint let out a roar of rage, and words spilled out of him. Why on earth would *he* have done such a thing? Hadn't he worked along with the rest of them? *He* hadn't gold-bricked like Chip — and he'd been just as crazy about the club as they were! Were they going to stand there and let that kid, that girl, get off a story like that, and *believe* her?

But it was all bluster. There was a way of telling. By his voice, somehow. And the way his eyes darted around. And the way his hands worked in his pockets. They didn't believe him. They couldn't.

Orphie said thoughtfully, "Come to think of it, fellas, that business of Chip's cap didn't mean a thing, either. He threw it down, remember, when he came in after he'd been to the movies? He always throws his cap on the floor. Only, this time, he left in such a hurry he didn't pick it up. Remember?"

Yes, they remembered. But Clint said, "He did have his cap with him when he went out. I saw him if you didn't. What's the matter with you guys?"

They were thinking sadly, What's the matter with Clint?

Mr. Randolph said heatedly, "It's nine to one against you, Clint. You can't get away with this."

Karl suddenly spoke up. "Maybe Clint was mad because we didn't make him president of the club. I know he's been telling a lot of the kids at Junior High that *he* was going to be the president when we got around to having one."

It was an idea. It must have hit the nail on the head, for Clint said rudely, "Yeah, and what did you do but elect that Bob Brown? And why?" He shook his fist at them. "Just because he had the caboose in his yard? Just because his uncle got him the caboose and the timetable and an engineer's cap? Is that any reason to make him president? You're a bunch of saps if you think I don't know why you did it. You make me sick!" And while they stood rooted to the floor, he brushed past them and slammed out of the front door.

"Well," said Bonnie, "I guess that's that. I've got to go back — I told Pat I'd be right back."

Bruce gave his sister a friendly shove. "Good work, Bonnie." Then she, too, was gone.

They apologized to Mr. Randolph. They apologized to Chip. Chip fished in his pocket, as they were leaving, and said dully, "Well — here's my key."

Bob said stoutly, "Keep it. You're back in, if you want to be, and you know it. Just see that you turn up at the next meeting."

And Skinny flung at him, "You can't blame us too much, Chip, for thinking it was you — after the way you acted lots of times."

Pete commented, "So you better turn over a new leaf if you don't want to get in trouble from now on."

147

Chip took it. He nodded gratefully. "Sure. I know. I'll be there."

Well, they thought, walking back slowly to the Browns, the mystery was solved. Thanks to Bonnie! It was awful that they had accused the wrong person.

Clint was out, of course. He had condemned himself. And Chip was back in. Maybe — who knows? — he would be a better member for all this.

But what to do about Bonnie? It was in all their minds.

"She sure helped us out! Boy, what a pickle! Pretty keen of her, wasn't it, to notice a thing like that?"

"She's helped us quite a few times, one way or another," Skinny admitted. "Remember how she showed me how to pick up those tiny springs for the couplers with a razor blade, when I was having the dickens of a time with them?"

"Yeah, and she taught me how to hold little pieces that had to be glued together, by using bobby-pins!"

"She had ideas about the wiring, too— quite a few ideas!"

"And now this," Bruce added, as if even he could hardly believe it.

Skinny said mournfully, "Oh, she's as good as any of us at the mechanical end of the pike."

"Of course we haven't got a constitution yet, but does this mean we'll have to put in it that girls can be members?"

"Gosh," Pete groaned. "Girls! One would be bad enough — even one could spoil things."

"But we're out a member, and we want to have ten. . . ."

148

"We could ask Vince Garland," Jan said eagerly. "He's crazy to join."

"But we've got to do something about Bonnie. I mean, she helped us so much and everything, and if we have a vacancy —"

Bob said dully, "Well, let's put it to a vote right here and now, before we get back."

They stopped in the middle of the road, lugubriously. It would be the end of the kind of good times boys could have together . . . but what could they do? If it hadn't been for Bonnie, they would be in the soup . . . and she had her uses. They guessed they could put up with her, and between them they might keep her in her place.

"All those in favor?" Bob asked. They all held up their hands, some only halfway. But they knew where their duty lay, and they did it. Nobody felt very happy, though.

Suzie was leading Doctor Quack on his airing around the yard, Rex cavorting beside her. Bonnie was chattering with Pat on the back porch steps. From the house wafted the good smell of roasting chicken. Everything looked about as usual around the Brown homestead, even to Kenny coming through the hedge, asking hopefully, "Can I go in the caboose with you? Can I?"

"The police have gone," Pat announced importantly. "They talked to us a lot, before they left. We don't know where they went — to Clint's house, maybe —"

Bob brushed that aside. He walked up to Bonnie and

149

stood in front of her solemnly. His throat felt dry; it was hard to bring out the words. Skinny gave him a poke.

"Uh — the Caboose Club members are mighty grateful for what you did, Bonnie," he said in a rush. "Helping us out with our pike, but most of all, keeping us from accusing the wrong guy. And we want to show you we really are grateful. So we — uh, we just voted —"

"Unanimously," Matt put in.

"Yes, unanimously — to ask you to become the only girl member of the Caboose Club. The dues," he hastened to add, "are twenty cents a week."

Bonnie's face flushed and her eyes widened. "Oh," she said, "oh, thanks." Their hearts went down to their shoes.

"But I think a boys' club should be for boys," she was saying. And she smiled at them. "Don't you?"

They all felt as if they would topple over. She was *refusing* to be a member! Was she in her right mind?

Not one of them was able to answer. Had they heard right?

"Don't *you?*" she repeated.

At that they shouted in a chorus, "You bet!"

Bob felt as if a great weight had been lifted from his chest. Looking around, he could tell the others felt that way, too. The Caboose Club was still their own.

"Come on, fellas," he called happily, "out to the club-house! There's a lot of work to be done!"